THE
BLACK SWAN

ALSO BY JEROME CHARYN

THE
BLACK SWAN

A Memoir

JEROME CHARYN

Thomas Dunne Books
St. Martin's Press
New York

THOMAS DUNNE BOOKS.

An imprint of St. Martin's Press.

Design by Heidi E.R. Eriksen

Library of Congress Cataloging-in-Publication Data

Charyn, Jerome.
    The black swan : a memoir / Jerome Charyn.—1st ed.
        p.   cm.
    Sequel to: The dark lady from Belorusse.
    ISBN 0-312-20877-4
    1. Charyn, Jerome—Homes and haunts—New York (N.Y.)
    2. Novelists, American—20th century—Family relationships.
    3. Bronx (New York, N.Y.)—Social life and customs.
    4. Charyn, Jerome—Childhood and youth.   5. Motion pictures—
    Appreciation.   I. Title.
    PS3553.H33 Z4615 2000
    813'.54—dc21
    [B]   00-025192

First Edition: June 2000

10

Faigele as a schoolgirl in Belorusse.

DELILAH

*Beauty, my phantom dog, gazing at Faigele,
not at me or Marve (right), who has all the sadness of
Belorusse in his eyes.*

live on a hill overlooking the Montparnasse cemetery, but a hill is not a home. It's where I camp out, like some bedouin, whose only comfort is the darkness of desert sand. I have a tutor. Lil. A woman who suffered during the war, watched her own parents whisked off the street and sent to that strange eternity of a Jewish camp, while Lil had to live like a waif, hide her red hair from the police. Lil is another homeless person who happens to have an address. That's why we get along.

I can't seem to grasp the myriad spiderwebs of French grammar, so we study Baudelaire and his *Spleen de Paris*, hoping that some of the master's demonic graces will rub off on me. Why do I feel closer to him than any other writer? Perhaps it's because Baudelaire is the first poet to describe the city not as an emblematic series of masks, gruesome *or* profoundly picturesque, but as a living thing that breathes its own special fire. He understands the *necessity* and the sadness of urban life, where all of us are driven by "an invincible need to march and march," searching for our very own chimera. . . .

I teach at a little university on the avenue Bosquet, talk about crime films and crime novels. Most of my students are wanderers like myself, misfits who probably couldn't thrive as well at another institution. Kids from Oklahoma, Istanbul, and Iran, who've come to Paris, sit in class with their nutty professor, who tells them that films belong to the night world of their dreams, that they themselves wear a cinematic face, like some chimera on a wall.

After my courses I catch a bus and climb off at Montparnasse. The cemetery is closed and I can't visit Baudelaire's tomb. It's my favorite pilgrimage in Paris. The tomb is tucked away, off the cemetery's little avenues. And Baudelaire's name is hidden on the tomb, sandwiched between his stepfather, General Aupick, and his mother, Caroline. Time has played its own dirty trick on the general. His glories are scratched into the tomb like a laundry list: senator, general, former ambassador to Constantinople and Madrid. . . . But he's only remembered now in relation to his sickly, impoverished stepson who suffered from aphasia.

I worry about my own aphasia. Sometimes I can't remember from moment to moment the words I write, as if language were taking revenge on a wild child from a little sand dune called the Bronx, at the other end of the world. My adulthood and identity seem to have collapsed into dust. My mother was an orphan from Belorusse. I miss the life she could have had if only she'd kept her promise and gone to school with me, from kindergarten to college. She might have become another Colette. But I'm the chronicler, losing language day by day. Each word Lil "lends" me cuts into my American vocabulary. A widow, Lil moves from one maid's room to the next, with her little bounty of books. She discovers that her latest address is a block from where her parents were snatched. Lil is like a somnambulist. . . . Her voyages across Paris bring her closer and closer to the irrevocable wound of her childhood. Pah! I don't want to learn French.

I shut my eyes and think of the pharmacies on every corner, with their twitching and twirling green and blue crosses that are like a psychedelic sign out of my own past, when giant posters of Gregory Peck would blink on some electric billboard attached to a moving truck. But these pharmacies are much more magical than any billboard. They have bandages and ankle guards and herb teas, syrups and potions that can bring the dead back to life. Is that why I live in Montparnasse, without the ghosts of Hemingway or Gertrude Stein? But I do have Jean Gabin. I remember him as Pépé le Moko, a caid who's trapped like a magnificent spider monkey in the Casbah. We can feel the *pain* of Paris in his eyes. "Paris, that's the dump where I used to live." Pépé's private hole in the wall.

And Paris is also my hole in the wall. I don't have a favorite haunt like the Dôme or Deux Magots. I eat at different dives with the restaurant tickets I get from my

little university. It gives a wanderer the illusion that he's
almost eating for free. But I didn't come to Paris to gather
tickets. Paris is where the bedouin boy has his tent, because
it does not tyrannize, impose its "aura" on you, make you
feel picturesque. Paris presents itself like a series of magnificent crime scenes. And perhaps we're all criminals playing out our perfect little parts, like Pépé le Moko in the
Paris of our dreams. I walk Paris like an invisible man,
while I live with the fantasms inside my head.

A single word breaks through these fantasms. *Luxor*, a
city along the Nile, and its temple of Queen Hatshepsut,
where fifty-eight tourists were shot and hacked to death by
Gamaa Islamya, a terrorist group, posing as policemen.
There's a distressing irony to the killers' disguise. Queen
Hatshepsut, Egypt's only female pharaoh, loved to put on
a beard and walk among her subjects, masquerading as a
man. But Hatshepsut brought delight, not butchery. And
the Luxor terrorists weren't cross-dressers, like the queen.

I had a "Luxor" of my own, a movie house off the
Grand Concourse. It wasn't much of a palace. It didn't have
Egyptian gods in the walls. My Luxor had a candy counter
and a dead beetle or two in its carpets, that's all. But it's
the only home I ever had.

How the hell did it happen? I was a nervous child,
caught between my mom and dad, their battles *and* their
reconciliations. We had a new baby in the house. Little
Marve. He was two years old in 1949. He'd already climbed

out of his crib. Dad was much gentler with him than he'd ever been with me.

My older brother, Harvey, was exiled to Arizona at a school for asthmatics. Harve was outside the stream of our lives. I was called "Baby" until little Marve arrived. Dad had meant to belittle me, hold me frozen in short pants. But Marve was the baby now. And dad seized my nickname . . . and my dog. Beauty. A Pomeranian–fox terrier who was the meanest little bitch in the Bronx. She would snap at me if I went near her. My dog. She was like a sister to mom. She would curl under mom's legs, follow her into the street. But Beauty disappeared when mom returned from the hospital with little Marve. Not a syllable was uttered about the little Pomeranian. I tried to worm the truth out of mom.

"Baby," she said. "We couldn't keep the dog."

"Why not, mom?"

And she started to cry. Mom was notorious in the Bronx. She'd once dealt cards for the Democratic Party. But she couldn't subscribe to the internecine wars. And the Democrats had banished her to the East Bronx, a land's end without a proper clubhouse or the least bit of patronage. She was still the most beautiful ex-dealer the Democrats had ever had. The dark lady from Belorusse, who was beginning to have a shock of gray in her hair. But no amount of gray could diminish her, make her less of a dark lady. And she missed *my* dog.

It was dad who unmasked the mystery. "Jerome," he said, "we had to get rid of her. Dogs aren't human. They can't control their jealousies."

"But . . ."

"She could have scratched Marve's eyes out, eaten off his nose."

"Did you give Beauty away?"

"No," he said, like a military man (dad had been an air-raid warden). "We had her gassed."

"Gassed my dog? You couldn't have lent her to a neighbor until Marvin grows up?"

"Impossible," dad said. "She would have died of misery. She was devoted to Faigele."

Faigele was mom's diminutive. It means "little bird." Her official name was Fannie.

Why did I lament? I didn't even like Beauty. I *hated* her. I would have drowned her in the bathtub if I could. But no one had the right to gas my dog . . . without my written consent. And I couldn't reconcile myself to dad's deadly arithmetic, that the birth of a little boy should produce a dog's end. I was powerless to alter such an equation. I took to Marve. I played with him. I mended the struts of his crib. I didn't have to endure any dog bites. But it was the principle of the thing. Beauty's death had *enlarged* her, made the bitch into some kind of Lassie, but *this* Lassie would never come home.

I lost my concentration. I was listless at school. My classmates began to mock me, call me "Dumbo," because

I had very big ears and I mooned around like a baby elephant. They wouldn't have dared call me Dumbo while Beauty was alive, because I was much more alert and would have tossed back their compliments with my own poisonous tongue. But I couldn't counterattack.

I stopped going to school. I didn't tell mom or dad. I would carry my briefcase around with me, keep regular school hours, but I'd wander off to the West Bronx, where we'd lived when mom had been a card dealer, and I'd sneak into that little movie house, the Luxor, just before noon, when the cashier drifted into his booth. The Luxor didn't have any ushers or usherettes to peer at me with a flashlight, and I had all the seats to myself.

Was it some weird accident or twist of fate that my first film at the Luxor was *Samson and Delilah* by Cecil B. De Mille? I fell in love with that giant from the land of Dan with hieroglyphics on his arm and the hair of a girl. Samson, otherwise known as Victor Mature. He was against the Philistines, who wore gold helmets and ruled over Dan. But the Philistines couldn't conquer Victor Mature without their own little agent, Hedy Lamarr.

There was never much confusion in my mind about actors and actresses and the roles they played. Hedy Lamarr was only "lending" herself as Delilah; I didn't have to take her too seriously as a Philistine spy with curly dark hair. And how could I forget Victor Mature as Doc Holliday, the gambler who couldn't stop coughing blood in *My Darling Clementine*, or as the small-time hood in *Kiss of*

Death, who gets caught between the law and Tommy Udo (Richard Widmark), the grinning gangster who became immortal in the Bronx after he hurled a grandma down a flight of stairs?

But *Samson and Delilah* was a little different. Mature was playing himself, a gentle giant on the verge of slumber (he could barely keep his eyes open on-screen), but the long hair gave him a touch of divinity, as if he were God's child, and the Philistines were only Philistines, fools in funny gold hats, while Delilah was a witch who fed Samson wine and got him to reveal the secret of his strength: his long, girlish hair. Delilah drugged him and cut his hair while the giant slept.

De Mille's Delilah is a very ambiguous girl. She didn't want the Philistines to butcher her favorite brute. They only blind him, cart him off to the prison house, where Samson is condemned to go round and round, pulling an enormous millstone, as he grinds grain for the Philistines. . . .

It's Hollywood. And Hedy Lamarr can't play a slut. She falls in love with the giant she tricked. His hair begins to grow. But the Philistines are much too blind to see that. Samson is their mule. Delilah visits him at the prison house. "Your arms were quicksand," Samson says. "Your kiss was death." But he can't stop loving Delilah.

The Philistines bring him into their temple, so they can mock the brute, and his invisible God, and show him off to Dagon, their own fire god, who had an enormous furnace of a mouth. But Samson pulls two of the main pillars apart, destroys the temple and all the Philistines, including Delilah, who doesn't want to live without her brute.

I couldn't stop crying. *Samson and Delilah* was like a cautionary tale of the Bronx. Samson could have been my own miraculous uncle or long-haired older brother, fighting Philistines from Manhattan (or Ohio), who happened to hate our little borough. After all, he was a Jewish giant, even if De Mille made the Danites seem like any old tribe.

I returned to the Luxor five days in a row. I didn't have to worry about letters from my public school. I was the family scribe. (Mom couldn't go to school with me and master the alphabet while she had little Marve, couldn't become Colette.) I answered all our mail. I knew how to forge my father's signature, and I was already dreaming up a letter in my mind, about having some chronic bone or brain disease. I was shrewd as Delilah. Or so I began to think.

On my sixth or seventh outing, I got caught. The Luxor seemed to have a Samson of its own. He plucked me out of my seat in the dark, while Delilah was on the screen, carried me across the theater, down a flight of stairs, and into a little cave, where my eyes had to deal with a sputtering fluorescent light.

There were two other men in the cave. The three of them must have been in their thirties, though it was hard for a kid of eleven to judge the exact age of adults, particularly when he'd come blinking out of the dark.

"What makes you so interested in Samson and Cecil B. De Mille?" said the Luxor's giant, who was as burly as Victor Mature. "We don't mind you sneaking in . . . but not every day."

"Should we give you an envelope, so you can claim the Luxor as your address?" said the second man, who was thin as a pencil and had a very pale face. The third man was quiet.

"I love Samson," I said. "And I live here between noon and three o'clock."

"Ah, so I was right," the second man said. "This is your address. You're a hooky player, aren't you? What's your name?"

"Jerome. But everybody used to call me Baby."

"Then we'll call you Baby," said the giant. He introduced himself as Everett Darling. The second man was Luke Goldberg. The third man, who was long and wiry, and had very beautiful lips, got out of his chair and slapped my face.

"I say we give him to the cops."

"That's brilliant," said Everett Darling. "We've been avoiding the cops for years. Should we invite them to the Luxor? Tell the kid you're sorry you slapped him."

"Suppose I slap him again."

"Then you'll have to face some thunder," said Luke Goldberg. "Ev and me will tear you apart."

"Apologize to Baby," said the giant.

"Bullshit."

"Then shake his hand and introduce yourself. We're not barbarians."

"I'm Murray Bell," said the third man, and shook my hand. "But you still haven't decided what we do with him."

"Nothing," said Luke Goldberg. "He's our guest."

"And we have to lose the price of a ticket to a hooky player?"

"We've been playing hooky all our lives," said Luke.

"That's different. We're professional hooky players."

"So's the kid. But he's just starting out."

"He's a snot nose. Only an idiot would see *Samson and Delilah* seven times."

"Did he have a choice? We haven't changed the bill in two weeks . . . but why'd you pick our theater, Baby?"

"Used to live next to the Concourse," I said. "On Sheridan Avenue. My mom dealt cards for the Democrats. Faigele Charyn. Did you ever hear of her?"

"No," said the Luxor's three cellar rats.

"She was famous for a little while. But she wouldn't vote for Franklin Roosevelt."

"Why not?"

"Because Roosevelt betrayed Darcy Staples."

"He talks a mile a minute," said Murray Bell, "and makes no sense. Who's this Darcy Staples?"

"A dentist. He was king of the Grand Concourse. Don't you guys ever leave the Luxor?"

"We're draft dodgers, if you have to know."

"You wouldn't fight the Germans and the Japs?"

13

"Japs?" Murray said. He was the only cellar rat who wore a stylish suit. I wondered if he went to Darcy's tailor, Feuerman & Marx, who dressed the classiest people in the Bronx. But Darcy never sneered the way Murray Bell did. "Japs? We wouldn't touch the Pacific. We've never been south of New Jersey."

"Stop that," said the thin man, Luke. "You're misleading Baby."

"He's too big to be called Baby. I'm calling him Jerome . . . what happened to your dentist?"

"He died in the Tombs. Of a broken heart. The Democrats sacrificed him, for Roosevelt's sake."

"Nobody dies of a broken heart," said Murray Bell.

"Darcy did."

"That's sentimental crap."

He was about to punch me in the face. But Everett trapped Murray's fist in his own paw.

"We're not real draft dodgers. We sat out the war. Luke has a little hole in his heart. The army would never take him. And it had to let Mur go."

Everett pointed to the photograph of a fireman on the wall. The fireman had blond hair and was holding a very big hook.

"Mur's fond of boys."

"That's none of Baby's business," Murray said.

"I still don't understand."

"He tried to make love to his own drill sergeant. The

sergeant put him in the hospital . . . the army doesn't like homos."

"Who's a homo? I'm an artiste."

And I looked at my Samson of the movie house, looked into his eyes. "What about you?"

"I'm a C.O.," he said. "I don't believe in rifles and bayonets. I spent six months in the Tombs . . . but I never met your dentist. I would have remembered him. Darcy Staples."

"He didn't last very long. He was too refined to live in a cell."

"And I'm too vulgar to die," Samson said.

The three cellar rats had been classmates at William Howard Taft, the Concourse's very own high school. They'd all lived at one or another of the Art Deco castles on the Concourse. Their dads were successful businessmen. Everett's was practically a tycoon. The rats had applied to Harvard, and all three got in. But they weren't very comfortable in the Ivy League, with its privileged clubs and professorial teas. They studied philosophy, but they seldom went to class. They flunked out of Harvard and had to find some other anchor. They weren't businessmen or philosophers. There was nothing in the world that could hold their curiosity. They pooled their resources, borrowed from their dads, and bought the Luxor, an ailing movie house. They hired a projectionist, a couple of cashiers, and sat in their cave, when they weren't watching whatever "vehicle" was on the screen. They could call themselves entrepreneurs, and they didn't have to thirst for anything beyond the Luxor's doors.

They were dropouts, three rats in a cave, without children or wives, but Everett had shares in IBM, shares that he sat on and could use as collateral if an unexpected bill arrived. He and Luke were in love with their former high school teacher, a certain Mrs. Green, who had aroused their interest in philosophy and art, encouraged them to go to Harvard. Perhaps it was Mrs. Green's *absence* from Cambridge, Massachusetts, that brought them back to the Bronx. She was slightly alcoholic, had a husband and two boys, and "lived" with Everett and Luke part-time at the apartment the three rats kept on Marcy Place, a stone's throw from the Luxor.

I was dying to meet Mrs. Green, but Everett had to discourage her from dropping in on them at the movie house.

"Baby, if she sees you, she'll send you back to school."

"But couldn't you say I'm a cousin visiting from Appalachia?"

"She'd know it's a lie. And we'd risk losing her. You're my little brother, but I'd have to break your neck."

"It isn't fair," I said. "You shouldn't deprive me of an interesting person. I'm a kid. I haven't met that many people."

"Shut up," the giant said. "That's final."

It was easy to invent a fable. When the letters did come from school, I'd scratch out a note in my father's hand, talk of fatigue, visits to a brain surgeon, etc. The East Bronx was like the Sahara, where a child and all his records could get lost in some infinite sand dune.

Did Faigele suspect anything? I'd leave the house early and come back as late as I could, swearing that I'd joined the glee club and was taking music lessons with an instrument that the school itself provided, which was at least half true. There must have been a craze for music education in 1949, and P.S. 61 lent out little plastic clarinets, hoping to find a genius or two in our part of the Sahara. These clarinets were unplayable. But a music teacher would arrive from the Board of Ed and instruct us how to blow on this horrid plastic thing. I could never negotiate more than a couple of toots. And I dropped out of music class after the third or fourth lesson. How could mom have known? She was occupied with little Marve. But she'd sensed the estrangement between us.

"Play for me, Jerome."

"Ah, mom, we do finger exercises."

"Play for me."

And so I tootled on that impossible clarinet, like the Benny Goodman of the East Bronx, and mom began to laugh. After that she left me alone.

I'd become an addict. I couldn't survive without the Luxor seven days a week. I had to maneuver on weekends, pretend I'd become the music teacher's prodigy and was getting private lessons at her home in the West Bronx.

"What's her name?" Faigele asked.

"Mrs. Green."

And I ran off to my three underground men. They finally changed the bill to *Twelve O'Clock High*, a war picture with Gregory Peck. But I couldn't watch it in peace. The cellar rats kidnapped me from the Luxor, brought me out to their Nash, a car that reminded me of a big fat bullet with a bump on its back. Everett was the navigator. He drove the Nash. Murray Bell sat up front with him. He was excited. His shoulders began to shake.

I sat with Luke. Something was wrong. Luke's eyes were clouding. He didn't even watch the window.

"Who invited Baby?" he asked.

Nobody answered him.

"Don't you get it? He's from Internal Revenue. The tax man can't trap us, so they send a kid."

The giant didn't even look at him. "That isn't logical, Luke."

"Sure it's logical. They have a training school for runts like him. J. Edgar Hoover started it."

"Hoover isn't with the IRS."

"He offered his services," Luke said. "He volunteered. He's a federal agent. If he helps the tax man, his own tax bill is cut in half . . . we have to get rid of Baby."

"Baby's one of us."

"I'll kill him myself."

I inched away from Luke. But I saw Everett's eyes in the mirror, and there wasn't the slightest alarm. I could swear he was signaling to me. He reached around and cuffed Luke on the forehead without taking his eyes off the wheel. The blow seemed to calm Luke.

"Baby," the giant said, in a voice that was half a whisper. "Empty your pockets, please."

I didn't have very much: the digger I liked to carry (it was my favorite top and could bite into asphalt with the most dramatic spin); the worn piece of string that went with the digger; and a clump of nickels I had for carfare.

"Luke," the giant said, "did you find a gold badge . . . or any other evidence of a tax man?"

"What about Baby's briefcase?"

I opened the briefcase and took out the plastic clarinet I needed for my phantom music lessons.

"It's a dud," I said. "A public school clarinet. Not even God could play it."

Luke picked up the clarinet, fiddled with the finger holes, and started to play "Irish Eyes Are Smiling." He could pull the sweetest tones out of that pathetic thing.

"Baby," he said. "It's not a clarinet. It's a cross between an ocarina and a kazoo."

I didn't argue. He'd soothed himself with his own song.

"Luke," the giant said, "did you take your medication?"

"No, Ev. I forgot."

"And what happens when you forget? Will I have to wallop you again?"

"No, Ev. I'll be good."

I wasn't a scientist. I didn't know anything about manic-depressive maniacs. But it was curious. Murray ignored the entire escapade. He looked out the window, searching for something. We got to a firehouse across from Claremont Park.

"Dan," he said. "I need Dan . . . will you tell that brat with the big ears to fetch him for me?"

"Baby doesn't have big ears," Samson insisted.

"Take another look. If you pitched him out the window, he'd start to fly. He comes right out of Walt Disney . . . Ev, I'm suffering. I'm gonna die without Dan."

And Everett told me about the blond fireman, Dan O'Brien, and his relation to the Luxor. There'd been a very suspicious fire at the movie house a year ago. Had the Luxor's landlord started that fire to collect insurance money and chase out the three underground men? It wasn't clear. But the three rats were trapped inside their cave, while the fire roared. The heat scorched their eyebrows. They stuffed wet handkerchiefs into their mouths to avoid breathing in the black smoke. They couldn't pray. The rats didn't believe in God. They started to hallucinate. The door shivered and fell in front of their feet. And a god did appear in a thick rubber coat. A blond god, with blue eyes, and a long hook in his hands. Dan O'Brien from Fire Company 42. All the smoke in the world couldn't damage his blue eyes or darken his smile.

"Gentlemen, hold on to that hook."

For Murray Bell it wasn't a matter of survival. He fell madly in love, went gaga over an hallucination in a rubber coat. He would have fainted from the beauty of that boy if Everett hadn't grabbed his hands and placed them on the fireman's pole.

Dan O'Brien led the three rats through a maze of burning pillars and broken glass and brought them out to the street. Murray couldn't take his eyes off Dan, who was twenty-two years old, the son of a fire chief.

Luke and Ev wanted to sell out, give that burnt theater back to the landlord, but they had nowhere else to go. And for Murray the Luxor had become a shrine: it was where he'd first met Dan O'Brien.

Murray wanted to court the fireman. "Ev, do you think he'll mind that I'm a fairy?"

"He'll break your bones."

So Murray had to limit his romance to stealing looks at Dan O'Brien from the window of the Nash.

"Couldn't I bake him cookies?"

"You never baked a cookie in your life. And you don't bake cookies for a fireman. It would embarrass him around his mates."

So the three rats would follow Dan O'Brien from fire to fire, snap his picture as often as they could. And I was their secret weapon. They'd never had a kid in their fraternity. I could approach Dan. Who would ever think that I was amorous of him?

"I'm not gonna do it."

"Baby," the giant implored. "Look at Mur . . . he'll drop dead in a minute. We're in a danger zone."

I got out of the car, muttering to myself. *I'm not Cupid, I'm not Cupid.* But I entered the fire company, asked the watchman inside the door if Dan O'Brien was there.

"And who's wanting him?"

"An admirer," I said. "Mr. O'Brien saved my uncle's life."

And the watchman screamed into an enormous foghorn. "Danny O'Brien, Danny O'Brien, you have a visitor, Danny-O."

The fire pole *instantly* began to shake. A man came riding down the pole in a blue T-shirt with the words EN-GINE 42 emblazoned on his chest. It was midwinter, and he had nothing on but the T-shirt, white socks, and a pair of pants. The rats hadn't been wrong about him. He was like a walking hallucination, with biceps, blue eyes, and a boyish smile.

He shook my hand.

"I'm Jerome," I said. "You rescued my uncle . . . about a year ago. At the Luxor fire."

"Luxor fire?"

"The movie house, next to the Grand Concourse."

"I remember now. I had to hack my way into the basement."

"Uncle's outside. He'd like to say hello . . . and thank you again."

The young fireman strode into the winter streets in his socks. Murray was mortified. He was sure I'd fail. He hadn't expected Dan O'Brien to slide down his pole and come to greet him. Everett had to shove Murray toward the window.

"Mur, aren't you going to say something to Fireman O'Brien?"

Dan's blue eyes must have twisted Murray's tongue. But he did climb out of the Nash. He was paler than Luke.

"Fireman," he said.

We all waited. What could we do?

"Brave, brave fireman."

He began to cry. And Dan O'Brien took Murray Bell in his arms, rocked him like a baby.

"Sir," Dan said. "It must have been an ordeal. I'd invite you inside the station. But you know how firemen are . . . like a private club. They're not privy to strangers."

Dan O'Brien said good-bye to us all and returned to Engine 42.

It wasn't the end of our trip. We crossed into New Jersey, Samson at the wheel. Murray Bell was dreaming of Dan

O'Brien. We didn't interfere with that dream. We stopped at a place called Union City. It was the capital of burlesque. I didn't know what burlesque was, except that it was outlawed in the Bronx. We arrived at the Tenderloin, which sounded like a steak to me, but it was a row of streets where sailors went. They flocked around theaters that had enormous billboards of half-naked women beckoning to the sailors with their backsides. I'd never seen such a spectacle. It was like traveling back through time, into the land of the Philistines.

We got out of the Nash. Murray retrieved a box from the trunk and painted a mustache under my nose, dabbed my eyes with a brush. I glanced at myself in Murray's mirror.

"What's this all about?"

"They don't let minors into the Martinique," Samson said.

"Then what am I supposed to be?"

"A very tall dwarf."

Samson put a cigar in my mouth, and we went into the Martinique.

"Where's Murray?" I asked.

"Minding the car."

The Martinique wasn't much larger than the Luxor. It was packed with sailors and college students and old men with raw, red noses and pink eyes. I couldn't find a lady among them.

A big fat announcer climbed up onto the stage, wheezing like a sick elephant. He started making jokes. I couldn't understand a word he said. But the audience laughed. And then he introduced the acts.

"From Pomona," he said, "the pom-pom girl, the delight of college campuses, Miss Teresa Taft. Let's give this lovely a big hand."

There was nothing lovely about Teresa Taft, the pompom girl. I couldn't bear to watch her undress. With each bit of unraveling she'd reveal a new world of wrinkles. Why had the cellar rats brought me here, stole me from the Luxor and *Twelve O'Clock High*? I was curious about Gregory Peck and the pilots he had to send out on bombing missions, half of whom wouldn't come back. I couldn't imagine a general as young as Gregory Peck.

The acts at the Martinique went on and on, and I almost sank into oblivion. Then Samson nudged me.

"Baby, don't fall asleep."

The announcer grabbed his microphone. "And now, for the first time on the Martinique's stage, from the city across the river, Delilah, the delicious one. Let's all give her a Bronx cheer."

The sailors whistled and clapped. The college kids jumped in their seats. The old men remained skeptical, peering out from the perimeters of their red noses.

Delilah came through the curtain, bold as a Philistine princess. I started to shake. It was Hedy Lamarr, with her silver bodice, her amulets, her arm bracelet. Was Cecil B. De Mille sending out his actresses on the striptease circuit? Delilah didn't have to undress. The sailors, the kids, the old geeks were mesmerized. She walked the length of the stage in silver sandals and her Philistine helmet of curly hair.

"Delilah," the audience shouted, "Delilah."

I wasn't dumb. I knew Hedy Lamarr wouldn't come to a hole in the wall in Union City, no matter what De Mille demanded of her. This Hedy Lamarr was a "female impersonator," a man who could dazzle you with the arms and legs and bodice of a woman.

"That's Murray," I said. "He isn't minding the car."

"Shhh," said Luke. "It's a command performance."

"You can't have a command performance without a king."

"You're the king. You brought Dan O'Brien out of his fire station. So Murray's thanking you in his own fashion. He invented Delilah on the spot . . . he's dancing for you, Baby."

"Does that mean he likes me now?"

"No," Luke said. "He'll never like you."

I thought of Queen Hatshepsut dressing as a man for her loyal subjects. Why couldn't Murray Bell do the reverse? But this wasn't Egypt. And we weren't near the Nile. This was a firetrap on the Jersey Palisades, without gods and goddesses. I was still grateful. And in the cramped kingdom of a child's heart, I wasn't watching a cellar rat in the middle of a masquerade. It was delicious Delilah, doing her dance.

DUBBIE

Dubbie at eleven, looking like a waif.

couldn't disappear every weekend, run to the Luxor, be with my mates, Samson, Luke Goldberg, and Delilah. Sometimes mom would include me in her plans, and I couldn't scream about clarinet lessons, or Faigele might have called my fictitious music teacher and discovered that there were no lessons to cancel. So I had to play along whenever mom visited her big sister, Rose, who lived even deeper in that Sahara of the East Bronx. Rose hadn't come to America with mom. She'd arrived much earlier from Belorusse, and there'd never been that closeness of touch—kissing, feeling, squabbling. But Rose's daughter, Dubbie, had a rare kind of instinctive love for mom, and was much, much more than a niece. Dubbie was the magical daughter mom had never had. They were always touching each other: as if a moving, caressing hand could become a song with all the power and depth that was missing from my clarinet.

Dubbie would sacrifice her high school friends for a Sunday with mom. And if Rose was distant, a couple of generations removed from little Jerome, Dubbie was like the sister I *should* have had. She wasn't Delilah. There was no ambiguity in her gaze.

"Jerome," she'd say, and she'd talk about Monroe High School, which was across the Bronx River and didn't have a single black student. That's how segregated the Bronx had become. Dubbie was president of her class at James Monroe and had tried to break this color barrier, but the principal wouldn't listen to her pleas. She wrote to Fred R. Lions, our borough president. All she got back was gobbledygook, how Lions couldn't interfere with "those lads from Livingston Street" (home and headquarters of the Board of Education).

Lions had once been on our map. Mom and I had met him when she was the dealer at Darcy's poker game. That rumpled little man had adored the dark lady, would have done anything for her ... until Lions and his boss, Ed Flynn, abandoned Darcy and let him rot in the Tombs. And mom ran from the Democrats and all their offers to set her up as the Democratic Party's poker queen at the Concourse Plaza.

But she wouldn't desert her favorite niece. And one Saturday morning we went on a pilgrimage to the Concourse Plaza, Fred R. Lions' permanent abode. He would dispense his patronage from a crimson chair in the lobby.

Mom wore a blue dress. She was thirty-eight years old,

and a little heftier after Marve was born. But people still mistook her for Joan Crawford's twin. Dubbie wore her Monroe sweater and brown bobby socks. She didn't have mom's Tartar cheekbones or the maddening beauty of Hedy Lamarr. She had short curly hair. But I was in love with her anyway. Harvey wasn't there. He was eating up the sun in Tucson. And Marve wasn't my soulmate. He couldn't have understood why I'd gone AWOL from public school. He was two years old and hadn't started to talk. Dubbie was different. I could talk to her. She'd never have betrayed me to the Philistines. . . .

Our little war party arrived at the Concourse Plaza. Mom had brought Marve in his stroller. In the old days we would have gone to the front of Fred R. Lions' line. But Faigele had lost her clout. We stood for hours, while the Bronx borough president saw the sycophants on his list. And finally he got to us, pretending that he had forgotten Faigele.

"Madam," he said, "I'm tired. I've shaken too many hands. How can I help you?"

But mom knew how to devil him, how to rip off that mask he'd decided to wear.

"Mr. Lions," she said, "have you been to Woodlawn lately?"

"Why would I go there?"

"To visit Darcy's grave."

The mask fell off. The left side of his mouth began to twitch. His desertion of Darcy had been the big disgrace of Mr. Lions' life. Darcy Staples, that dentist and black marketeer, had forced the borough to recognize Fred R. Lions and treat the Bronx's own bagman with dignity.

"Faigele," he said, "are you making trouble again? I could have you thrown out of the hotel."

"Ah, my little prince, is this how you treat one of your constituents?"

"You're not a constituent," he said. "You're a black sheep. You've been outlawed from the Grand Concourse . . . is this Baby? Why does he have such big ears?"

"Because he's copying from Clark Gable," mom told him.

"And the toddler?"

"Marvin," she said. "My latest."

"What about the cheerleader?"

"My niece. Dubbie Yellin. She's not a cheerleader, Mr. Lions. She's president of her class. At James Monroe."

And the rumpled little man coughed into his fist. Not even a crimson chair could ennoble him in the least. He was lost without Darcy Staples, and he'd never know it. Darcy had done his thinking, given him a bit of allure, turned him into some sort of prince, in spite of the rumpled clothes. He'd thrived during Darcy's reign; now he was a functioning factotum.

"James Monroe," he muttered, "James Monroe." He'd remembered Dubbie's letter. "I'm not God. Can I shift the population around? Can I move the colored people across the Bronx River?"

"I wouldn't ask that of you," Dubbie said. "But you could let the boys and girls of Boston Road into Monroe?"

"They have their own high school. Gouverneur Morris. It's a gorgeous place. Like a castle."

"For colored kids," Dubbie said.

"But I don't set the districts, young lady. You give me too much credit."

"You could bite the mayor's ear," Faigele said.

"Me? I'm almost retired. Hardly ever go to the Bronx County Building. I do most of my business from this red seat."

"Then do," Faigele said.

"I can't. The Democratic clubs would start to holler. And the Board of Ed would laugh at me. I mean nothing to Livingston Street, nothing at all . . . Faigele, wouldn't I help you if I could? I have the dearest memories of our poker games with the dentist. Please say good-bye."

But the dark lady said nothing. I wheeled Marve out of the Concourse Plaza, with Dubbie and Faigele up front.

She wasn't always such a crusader. Dubbie had boyfriends who would track her right to her door. She was nearsighted, and no Linda Darnell, but she could make you laugh. Dubbie would walk with you into any danger.

She was working on a senior project about the Bronx as an "archipelago." That was a wondrous word. It sounded like an island filled with bald angels. But the Bronx wasn't an island. I'd learned that at school. It was the only borough that was part of the mainland, a real piece of America. But Dubbie insisted that the Bronx had an island culture, that it was an enclave like no other enclave. That it was its own Singapore, or Bali, with active volcanoes, underground rivers, and endless cafeterias, where, she said, "the lava of human milk liked to flow."

Our cafeteria was called the Chesterfield, which was right under the elevated tracks, at the juncture of Southern Boulevard and Boston Road. It was the land of perpetual darkness, because only ravaged bits of light could ever filter through the colossal carcass of an "el" station. And so the citizens of the Chesterfield, who spent their days and nights in a cavern as big as a football field, lived without sunlight on their cheeks, the "bald angels" of that archipelago I'd conjured up from Dubbie's dream.

You couldn't enter without taking a ticket from a machine. And if you wanted to eat at the Chesterfield, you would point to a bowl of Jell-O or a piece of lemon cake behind a counter that ran along the entire left wall, and the counterman would punch your ticket, which was like a primitive slate board with prices that ascended from a nickel to five dollars: an angel's abacus.

Dubbie and I took the tickets, but we hadn't come to eat; we ordered the minimum, a five-cent cup of coffee for her and a celery tonic for me. There was nothing in this world like celery tonic: soda water mingled with a celery solution that was supposed to relax your nerves and cure whatever stomach ailment you might have. I didn't have a stomach ailment. I suffered from nervous tics, known as "habits." I'd cough and have to keep clearing my throat, and if I got excited, my nose would twitch like a weasel or a rabbit. But I was perfectly calm at the cafeteria.

Dubbie was looking for Farouk. Every cafeteria had a sultan or caid, some mystery man who ruled the premises from a far corner, where no window could catch his reflection. Farouk was born in the Bronx. He wasn't a jewel thief, like Pépé le Moko, with a small army of accomplices. He was only a fat man who happened to bear a certain resemblance to Egypt's boy-king.

The real Farouk should have been unpopular in the Bronx. That boy-king welcomed the Nazis during World War II, sat on Egypt's throne when the Arabs attacked Israel in 1948. But *our* Farouk was devoted to the boy-king. The Chesterfield was the one cafeteria in the Bronx that had King Farouk's picture all over its walls. It infuriated the Chesterfield's Jewish clientele, particularly the bookkeepers and minor gangsters who belonged to the Little Man, Meyer Lansky. Lansky had contributed money and matériel to the Haganah and other secret armies that had battled the British before the creation of Israel. He was threatening to burn down the Chesterfield if our Farouk didn't take the boy-king's picture off the walls.

But Farouk was the caid here, not Meyer Lansky. He wouldn't negotiate with the Little Man. He had Lansky's loyalists kicked out of the cafeteria, and the Chesterfield continued to thrive in that dark web under the elevated tracks. Farouk didn't have hundreds of soldiers, like Lansky. He had a single bodyguard, a black man with a little beard, Tyrone Wood, who'd graduated from Gouverneur Morris. Tyrone had a thin, skeletal face. He wasn't tall, but he could impose his will on any stranger who tried to get near Farouk.

And the Bronx Egyptian who'd never been near Egypt had a ton of seekers, men, women, and children who'd come to the cafeteria to beg about *something*: a son who needed an operation, grandmas who couldn't pay the rent. Fred R. Lions' retinue at the Concourse Plaza was picayune compared to the pilgrims at the Chesterfield. Lions' hand couldn't reach into the East Bronx. He was no caid. He was the lackey of Boss Flynn. But at least we'd had an audience with Lions, thanks to Faigele. We couldn't approach Farouk's table.

And then our luck floated into the cafeteria in the form of Everett Darling, my Samson and cellar rat. He didn't have to join those other pilgrims. Gently, very gently, Tyrone Wood shoved the pilgrims to one side and opened a path for Samson to Farouk.

I wasn't blind. I saw Ev hand Farouk a fat envelope packed with paper money. And I could feel a lightbulb glow around my head, like it did in my comic book collection, when Captain Marvel had a brainstorm. Farouk was revealed to me in a flash. I knew the source of his strength, and it wasn't in his hair. *He* was the Luxor's landlord, and Samson had come to pay the rent.

They chatted, smoked little cigars called Fatimas. I watched the Bronx Egyptian laugh. Then Samson left Farouk's cortege. He was smiling until he saw me. The Fatima wiggled in his mouth.

"Baby, what are you doing in the king's cafeteria?"

"It's my cafeteria too," I said. "I have to meet with Farouk."

"If you're borrowing dollars, you should have asked me first."

"Ev, this is Dubbie. She's dying to interview the king. She wants to ask him if the Bronx is a real archipelago or not."

He squinted at my cousin. "What can Farouk tell her?"

"He's the sultan of the Bronx, isn't he?"

"Baby," Samson said, "he sits in a cafeteria day and night. He has no sense of the seasons. Summer and winter's the same to him. He hasn't been to a movie in years. He never even heard of Richard Widmark or Coleen Gray."

"He's still the sultan of the Bronx."

Everett shook Dubbie's hand, tapped Tyrone Wood on the shoulder, and brought us over to Farouk's table. Farouk was drinking celery tonic out of a gigantic glass. Samson vouched for me, said I was the Luxor's most loyal patron.

"And who's the little sweetheart?" the sultan asked.

"Baby's cousin. A scholar at James Monroe."

And Samson left us there, in the sultan's hands, marched out of that great big cavern with the Fatima like a glowworm in his mouth.

Farouk made the supreme gesture of intimacy at the cafeteria. He invited us to sit down with him and share his celery tonic. But there was so much noise from the other pilgrims, who barked their songs of misery, that Farouk obliged them to scatter from his table.

"Super," he said. "Now I can hear myself."

But Dubbie wasn't coy. She didn't play up to a cafeteria king.

"Mr. Farouk, how much do you grab from the Bronx on any given day?"

"As much as I can. But is this cafeteria the center of your research? Because I'm flattered. I've had assistant district attorneys nosing around. I've had Meyer Lansky's lads. But never a high school girl."

"Your Highness," I said, "she's president of her class."

"Then I'm doubly flattered. Fame is such a fickle thing. I'm notorious, and I haven't been outside this cafeteria in years, except for a couple of court dates. I sleep in the back room."

Dubbie winked at him. "Then I could call the Chesterfield an archipelago, with its own culture, wouldn't you agree?"

"If you include celery tonic," said the sultan.

"Mr. Farouk, you're toying with me."

"Not at all, miss. A cafeteria is defined by its beverages.

And the mark of the Chesterfield is celery tonic. That's what I drink. And that's what the cafeteria stocks. The company that supplies us is in Queens. I told them, 'That's not near enough. Suppose there's a strike on the Triborough Bridge?' They opened a Bronx branch. In the cafeteria's kitchen. You could accuse me of nepotism. But you would be wrong. I was seeking quality control. You know how jealously Coca-Cola guards its formula. It's the same thing with celery tonic."

"Then you're a profiteer. You manufacture and devour your own product and force others to devour it."

"That's unkind. It's the most beloved drink in the Bronx. Baby, what's your favorite beverage?"

"Celery tonic."

"Admit it," Dubbie said, "it's made you a millionaire."

"You're missing the point. I couldn't survive without celery tonic. I don't have an active life. It cleans the blood, soothes the bowels. I'm entitled to a profit."

"Then we are an archipelago. And it's a perfect example of Bronx capitalism."

"Of course," said the sultan. "Isn't that why you came to me?"

He shut his eyes. And the audience was over. The sultan had to sleep.

I wasn't greeted with much kindness when I got back to the Luxor. The rats had locked the door of their cave. So

I watched *Twelve O'Clock High* all the way through, suffered with Gregory Peck, Brigadier General Frank Savage of the 918th Bomb Group. It's 1943. And the young general has to fly with his men on the first daylight precision bombing over Germany. But the war begins to wear him down. He becomes a kind of twentieth-century Christ, absorbs the agony of his men, cannot bear it when the planes don't return from a mission. We can almost feel a slight twist in his face. And then he cracks. He cannot climb into his plane before a mission. His body betrays him. His own men have to carry him back to headquarters. He sits in a trance during the raid. The camera closes in. I was frightened for Gregory Peck. But his face untwists when he hears the grinding motors of the 918th. We know that he will never lead his men on another mission, that he's been washed out of the war.

I would have watched *Twelve O'Clock High* all over again, but Samson picked me up by the seat of my pants and carried me into the cave. My three underground men were furious.

"Baby," Samson said, "what did you tell your cousin about me?"

"Nothing much."

"Did you mention all of us?"

"Is it a crime? I said I had three friends who left Harvard to manage a movie house."

Luke started to choke me. Delilah slapped my face. Samson had to separate them.

"Is she going to come here and interview us?"

"She doesn't know the Luxor's address."

"We can't be part of any interview," said my Delilah, Murray Bell. "We're not supposed to exist. We're not on file. We don't have social security numbers. We've never paid any income tax."

"What about Farouk?" I said.

"Farouk's gone public. The government knows where to find him. Farouk was in the war. He won the Medal of Honor."

"You mean he left the cafeteria to fight the Germans?"

"The Japs," Samson said. "He was with Skinny Wainwright on Bataan."

"Who's Skinny Wainwright?"

Those cellar rats looked at me with contempt.

"Skinny was the greatest general in the war against the Japs."

"Greater than Douglas MacArthur?"

"MacArthur was a showboat general. He deserted Skinny, left him to hold the Philippines. Skinny was captured on Corregidor . . . with King Farouk. The Japs sent all their American prisoners on a death march. They weren't supposed to survive. Farouk was a skeleton at the end of that march. He weighed ninety pounds. He ended up with Skinny at a prison camp in Manchuria. And when he came home, he started to eat, and he's never stopped."

"He's your landlord, isn't he?"

"Shut up. We couldn't have rented the Luxor without King Farouk."

"But he almost killed you. He tried to burn you alive."

"He thinks too much," said Luke. "And sometimes his thoughts get violent."

"Who was he before he became Farouk? What was his name?"

"He was always Farouk."

"But on the death march . . . with Skinny Wainwright?"

"We didn't know him then," said Luke.

There was a knock on the cellar door.

"I'll demolish you," Delilah said, "if that's your little cousin . . . ask who it is?"

"Who is it?" I squawked, with Delilah's fingers on my throat.

"Open," a voice said from the other side of the door. "It's Tyrone."

The cellar rats were startled. King Farouk's bodyguard had never come to the Luxor. They had to let him in.

"Forgive me," Samson said. "We don't have celery tonic."

"Never touch the stuff. Gives me gas."

The giant started to twitch. "Was I short?"

"What you mean, Brother Ev?"

"The envelope . . . did I miss a couple of dollars?"

"The envelope's fine. The king took a liking to Brother Jerome."

42

"The little hooky player?" Delilah said.

"Hush," Tyrone said. "The king's partial to Jerome. We'd like to borrow him."

"What for? He's useless. He watches the same film over and over again."

"That's what makes him attractive to the king."

"Borrow him," Samson said. "See if I care."

But Samson did care. I'd become part of the furniture. I was the Luxor's property now.

"I'll bring him back," Tyrone said. And he whisked me out of the cave. I had to shield my eyes against the blinding winter sun. I was like a bat who could only live in one kind of cave or another. I sat up front with Tyrone in a black Hudson big as a boat. I didn't have to worry about the light. Tyrone's Hudson had tinted glass. He let me steal a puff or two off his Fatima. We drove "downtown" to the Hub, which was the heart of the Bronx's shopping district, located around the gigantic crossroad of Willis, Third, and Westchester avenues, and East 149th, under the Third Avenue el. If Manhattan had Macy's, we had Hearn's. But the Hub didn't have a cafeteria like the Chesterfield. It didn't have King Farouk.

Tyrone parked his Hudson in a no-parking zone. Traffic cops saluted him. The sultan's power must have extended to the Hub, even if he'd exiled himself to a cavern in one of the uptown fingers of the Bronx.

We got out of the car. "Where we going, Tyrone?"

"To get you a suit."

"A suit?" I said. "Didn't those draft dodgers tell you? I'm a hooky player."

"Only part of the time. You're collecting bills for the king."

"Why me?"

"He likes your manner. And I scare people. I'm too direct."

We marched to that mecca, Feuerman & Marx, where the dentist who was lying in Woodlawn had bought his hats, ties, and suits. It wasn't crowded, like the other stores along the Hub, because Feuerman & Marx wouldn't accept any old customer off the street. Feuerman & Marx selected its clientele. It was on the second floor of a warehouse devoted to furniture. We didn't have to enter the warehouse. Feuerman's stairs were outside the building, like a fire escape. The stairs were metal and had little diamond-shaped designs on each step. We could have been walking up to paradise.

The salesmen were expecting us. They'd come from London, the original home of Feuerman & Marx.

"Is this the young gentleman, Mr. Wood?"

"Indeed it is," said Tyrone.

"And how urgent is the fitting?"

"Totally urgent. He has to walk out wearing his suit."

"Ah, then we'll advise the tailor."

And they went to work on me, four men with measuring tapes and pieces of chalk. They kept pins in their mouths. They covered me with different material until Tyrone nodded yes to a particular piece of cloth, and then they stuck their pins in me, chalked me up and down, sang to themselves, summoned the tailor.

"How's King Farouk, if I may ask?" sang the chief salesman, Mr. Fox.

"Surviving," said Tyrone.

"We'd appreciate another five cases of celery tonic."

Tyrone took out a scrap of paper and scribbled something with a pencil stub. And I realized that the sultan was like a bootlegger. He trafficked in celery soda. The Chesterfield must have functioned as a distillery.

I tugged the salesman's sleeve. "Sir," I said, "are you the one who dressed Darcy Staples?"

He wouldn't answer.

Tyrone had to intercede.

"Jerome's asking you a question, Mr. Fox?"

"And I don't have to answer riffraff from the Bronx. Feuerman is the clothier of princes and kings."

"And my king will be delighted to hear that, since Jerome has been put in charge of distributing celery tonic."

"That's a different matter," said Mr. Fox. "But somehow I can't bring myself to remember this Darcy Staples."

Tyrone lit a Fatima and blew smoke rings in Mr. Fox's face.

"Curious, considering that Darcy Staples and his men policed this borough from the Concourse to the Hub."

"Policed it for whom?"

"The Democratic Party."

"Then that's the answer," said Mr. Fox. "I never get involved in politics . . . and it must have been before my time."

"Mr. Fox, there was no Feuerman before your time."

I was feeling very down. Darcy wouldn't have gone into the street without some bit of clothes from Feuerman & Marx. And the store couldn't even show its gratitude.

"I'll be right back," said Mr. Fox.

We had to wait for half an hour.

He returned with my custom-tailored suit, which wasn't showy or anything. It had gray stripes. I didn't want to wear it.

"Put it on," said Tyrone. "We're in a hurry."

Mr. Fox fitted me with a white shirt, a polka-dotted tie and matching display handkerchief, black socks, black shoes, and a black homburg. He bundled up my old clothes in a Feuerman box. Tyrone paid him in cash.

"Would the young gentleman like to look at himself in the mirror?" asked Mr. Fox.

"No," I said. "We're in a hurry."

I wouldn't shake his hand.

We climbed down the steps.

"Don't be too harsh on him," Tyrone said. "He's a salesman. He has to be selective about who he remembers. He does business with the Democrats. And those pashas would rather forget Darce."

"Did you know the dentist, Tyrone?"

"I did. I worked for the man. During the war."

"When Farouk was on that death march with Skinny Wainwright?"

The sultan's bodyguard rolled his eyes. "Those Luxor boys shouldn't have told you about Bataan and Corregidor. The boss doesn't like to reminisce about his days as a soldier. Might give people a bad impression. That he was too patriotic to run a cafeteria and sell celery tonic."

"Tyrone," I said, "I never saw you at the dentist's poker games."

"I was there . . . in the background. Whispering on the telephone. He had the sweetest dealer. A dark-haired bitch."

"She's my mom," I hurled at Tyrone.

He clapped his hands. "Baby, I didn't mean to show you disrespect. Darce was in love with her. We all were. Were you the little pisser in short pants who sat on a tall chair?"

"Tyrone, what exactly did you do for the dentist?"

"What you think? The usual stuff. I was Darcy's bill collector."

"Did you guard him like you guarded Farouk?"

"Didn't have to. Meyer Lansky wasn't after the dentist."

"I hate Lansky," I said. "His henchmen crippled my super, Haines. It's a long story. Haines was trying to protect one of mom's old admirers, who got in the Little Man's way . . . aren't you scared?"

"Of Meyer?"

"Didn't he promise to burn down the cafeteria with you and the sultan inside?"

"That's public relations," Tyrone said. "Meyer wouldn't dare touch the Chesterfield. He's a member of B'nai Brith. And the Brith would outlaw him if he started messing up colored people. That's a Jewish thing."

"But Haines is colored."

"Then it must have been before Meyer joined the Brith. He can't afford the bad publicity. He wants to be president of Israel, I think . . . or become a general, with his own brigade."

"I wish he'd die," I said.

And Tyrone laughed. "He will . . . one of these days."

We made our first stop, a delicatessen on Tiffany Street.

"Tyrone, what am I supposed to do?"

"Be natural. You're the king's new tax collector."

"I'm a kid," I said.

"In a Feuerman suit. That's all the credentials we need."

Tyrone shoved the homburg over my left eye. We entered the deli. Tyrone didn't even have to introduce me. The homburg spoke. I looked in the mirror. The dotted handkerchief was a dream. I scared myself. I could have been young Darcy Staples.

The owner of the deli grabbed my hand. "You're a hard bargainer, dear boy. But don't starve us . . . Farouk was a case short last week. We ran out of celery soda."

"But there's always Dr. Brown's," I said. That was the *other* brand.

The owner pinched my cheek. "Listen to him. Pushing the competition . . . my customers don't want Dr. Brown."

"Baby," Tyrone said. "Will you guarantee the delicatessen?"

I wasn't sure what to do. I shook my head, and then the deli man gave me a brown bag stuffed with dollar bills.

I walked out of there with Tyrone.

"I still don't get it. The full Feuerman treatment. You told me yourself. You were Darcy's collector."

"This is different. I cracked skulls for Darcy. The delicatessens shiver when I come in alone. But you . . . you're silk. You calm their nerves."

"Like celery tonic."

I slaved like a dog. I never realized how many delicatessens there were in the Bronx that carried Farouk's "product." But it wasn't only delicatessens. We stopped at movie houses, like the Kent and the Dale, where I also had to collect. And with each collection I understood the sultan a little more. He couldn't touch the chains, like the Loew's Paradise or the RKO Chester. The chains had their own unions and protection rackets, reinforced by the Hollywood moguls and their own mob princes, including Lansky. But Farouk was master of the independent movie houses. He'd carved his own little theater of operations in the tortured archipelago of the Bronx. Celery tonic. A cafeteria. Movie houses off the main boulevards . . .

I showed up at the Chesterfield with enormous money bags. The sultan didn't even say thanks. He handed me a wrinkled five-dollar bill. Starvation wages, the salary of a kid coming out of some Bronx labor camp. I didn't complain. He was just like any other tycoon, who could be generous *and* stingy according to his own will.

He must have thought that an outfit from Feuerman & Marx was enough compensation. But it was only a phantom suit. I had to keep it at the cafeteria. If Faigele caught me wearing a Feuerman, she would have guessed that I was up to no good. And the suit itself would have saddened her, made her think of Darcy. The dentist had never declared his love for Faigele, but he'd told another one of her admirers that Faigele was the only woman he'd have ever married, if she hadn't already been married to my father, Sergeant Sam, the ex-warden. Ah, it was a complicated business, this love and hate that grown-ups had for each other. De Mille captured a tiny portion of it in *Samson and Delilah.*

Farouk had driven a wedge between me and my cellar rats. They were cautious around the sultan's little champion. He'd given me free passes to the Kent and the Dale and all the other movie houses that were in his dominion. I preferred the Luxor. And when I wasn't slaving for him, I'd watch *She Wore a Yellow Ribbon* and *The Great Gatsby* with Alan Ladd. But Samson kept plucking me out of my chair.

I'd have to sit in the cellar and listen to the rats, who no longer trusted me. I begged Murray Bell to take me across the river to that burlesque house, the Martinique, and do Delilah again.

"I've dropped Delilah," Murray said. "Pulled her out of my repertoire, thanks to you."

"But Mur," I said, "you were much better than Hedy Lamarr."

He was still mourning his fireman, Dan O'Brien, from Engine 42, whom he couldn't visit in Delilah's clothes, because firemen didn't have much use for female impersonators. If anyone from Engine 42 had recognized Murray under his wigs and paint, the whole fire company would have torn him apart. So he was destined to suffer, since he couldn't reveal his own curious affliction to the love of his life.

And I became the target of his woes.

"You ruined it for us, Baby. Farouk will toss us into the street and let you have the Luxor."

But a letter arrived from the sultan himself, inviting the three underground men to a party at the Chesterfield, celebrating the fourth full year of his association with the cafeteria.

I didn't receive a letter from Farouk. He invited me in person after one of my collections across the Bronx.

"Baby," the sultan said, "invite whoever you like . . . but all I hear about is your mother's beauty."

I couldn't invite Faigele. She would have sensed my closeness to the sultan and understood that my afternoons and evenings had nothing to do with a clarinet. But I invited Dubbie, because she hadn't finished her research and she'd never have squealed on me. She brought her boyfriends with her, half the James Monroe basketball team, giants who were bewitched by her brains and curly hair. We all sat at an enormous table in the depths of the cafeteria.

The Chesterfield had shut its doors to the usual citizens of Southern Boulevard and Boston Road and turned off the ticket machine. The counter itself was closed, and the countermen served as waiters, wearing red Russian shirts that reached below their knees. They brought food to the sultan and his guests on enormous trays that they balanced on their shoulders. I tasted caviar for the first time in my life. I didn't enjoy it at all. It was like colored dots stuck in beeswax.

I don't know why the sultan sat Dubbie and me next to him. We couldn't have been as important as the partners in his distillery. He'd banished Everett, Luke, and Murray to the far end of the table. I couldn't find Tyrone. Farouk must have sent him on a mission. He seemed morose.

"Now is the winter our discontent," he whistled through his teeth. No one could answer him but Dubbie herself.

"My Lord," she said, "do dogs bark at you? Are you

rudely stamped? Deformed, unfinished, sent before your time into this howling world?"

The sultan's moroseness began to lift.

"Dubbie," I whispered, "what the hell are you talking about?"

"Shakespeare," she said. "Richard the Third."

"Who's this Richard?"

"A king with a lame arm and a hump on his back who kills everybody around him until he's killed because he can't find his horse."

"But Dubbie . . ."

"Shhh," she said.

Farouk had the audience he needed now: Dubbie Yellin.

"A horse," he shouted, "my kingdom for a horse."

His lackeys, the cafeteria people who depended on him, were dumbfounded. Even Samson, who had a high school diploma, scratched his head. "Farouk," he howled, "you can't have a horse in a cafeteria, or can you?"

Farouk wouldn't answer him. He plunged into his food. I'd never seen a man eat like that. He shoveled pickles and hot pastrami into his mouth. He burped and swallowed a mug of celery tonic.

"King," said another lackey, "you'll damage your heart."

The sultan ate and ate, like a wounded wolf grabbing whatever was in reach. A third lackey spoke. Farouk slapped his ears back. And after that, no one dared admonish him. But I was the sly one. I listened. I couldn't forget the bondage of a wrinkled five-dollar bill.

Farouk would only speak to Dubbie, and between mouthfuls. "Miss, I wouldn't be alive without Richard the Third. That hunchback was my savior. I learned the play by heart."

I let a little venom drop.

"Farouk, was that in Corregidor . . . or in Manchuria with Skinny Wainwright?"

The pleasure had gone out of his eyes. I'd forced him to lose his appetite. He clutched a chicken leg in his bare hand, and I wondered if he was going to fling it at me. I didn't flinch. It was like poker in the dentist's back office, with hot wires sizzling over each player's chair. But hadn't I watched the dark lady deal? Darcy had prepared me for bluffing, and a world of high stakes.

"Baby," he said, "you know about the death march?"

"You were ninety pounds at the end of it."

"More like eighty."

His appetite had come back. He bit into the chicken leg. "I was a lowly lieutenant. But the captains and the colonels were dropping like flies. They dreamt of food, and their bodies wasted. They undressed women in their minds. They died with Betty Grable and Greer Garson in front of them, like a mirage. Skinny said, 'Think of nothing, nothing at all.' That's how I survived, Mr. Baby Charyn."

I lifted up my glass of celery tonic. "To nothing," I said.

"But it was different in Manchuria. They put us in bamboo cages. And you couldn't afford an idle mind. Your eyes would glaze in their sockets. Skinny knew that. 'Play Marco Polo.' That was the message he sent down to us from his stinking cage. The others didn't understand. But I did. We had to become adventurers, travel and dream as hard as we could. Become bolder than the cages we were in. I dreamt of meals I'd prepared, the greatest chef on earth. Truffles and birds' eggs soaked in wine. I dreamt of Paris, imagined the pitch of a street. I walked Pigalle and the Latin Quarter, pictured myself as the Phantom of the Opera frightening German officers to death by shucking off my mask and showing them the horrible sores on my face. But how many Nazis could I kill without the flavor of it wearing off? So I turned to the Hollywood pantheon. Garbo. Dietrich. Joan Blondell . . . have you ever been with a woman?"

"Farouk, I'm only eleven."

"That elixir lasted for a month. The sweetness of a thigh. The nape of a neck. But soon all the bodies began to blend. And I was worse off than I'd been before I had Garbo and Dietrich. I was a goner. I had nowhere else to explore. I smuggled a note to Skinny. 'General, sir, can you give me some more ammunition?' Bless that man. He was a god and a general. I waited. I despaired. And then a Nipponese captain appeared in front of my cage with his ceremonial sword. I was hoping he'd finish me, cut off my head. But he dug a little book into the bamboo. Some cheap edition of Shakespeare for Jap officers who wanted to prepare themselves for the invasion of America and Mother England. Mine was Richard the Third. I couldn't stop crying. Baby, I had everything. Words, words, words."

Tyrone suddenly appeared like a ghost, cupped his hand, whispered to Farouk. The sultan smiled. "We have no secrets from Baby . . . or Miss Yellin. The Little Man was preparing to ruin my party. He made plans. He was going to smuggle in some goons, dress them as waiters, explode a little bomb. Kidnap me if they could. Nothing original. He wanted to humiliate me in my own cafeteria. But the Little Man is too visible. He can't keep it a secret when he goes shopping for goons."

"Farouk, are they dead?"

"Baby, Baby, I'm not King Richard. Tyrone hid them in a cellar somewhere."

"Does that cellar happen to be inside a movie house like the Luxor, for example?"

Tyrone nudged Farouk. "Boss, the kid knows me like a book."

"What do you expect? You trained him, sent him to your private college."

Farouk hummed to himself. He'd outsmarted the Little Man. But the humming stopped. His glory shriveled when he saw a woman with a little gray in her hair come into the cafeteria with a two-year-old boy in a stroller. Dubbie must have invited mom. She wasn't wearing lipstick or mascara. She had the silver fox coat that was a relic of World War II. Farouk looked at mom, then at me. He couldn't have avoided the cheekbones and Tartar eyes of Belorusse. Even with the weight mom had put on, she could dazzle a cafeteria.

"I'm cold," Farouk said.

Tyrone had put his own scarf around the king.

Farouk hugged himself. He started to babble Shakespeare, with one eye on the dark lady from Belorusse. I had to strain a bit to hear him.

"Your beauty," he said, "which did haunt me in my sleep . . ."

"Boss," Tyrone asked, "what's that?"

"Shhh. Don't interrupt . . . haunt me in my sleep, haunt me in my sleep, to undertake the death of all the world, so I might live one hour . . . in your sweet bosom."

"Dubbie," I whispered, "what's Farouk talking about?"

"Lady Anne."

"I don't see Lady Anne in the cafeteria."

"But you see Richard," she said.

"Shakespeare," I muttered, "in the Chesterfield insane asylum."

"Richard has widowed Anne twice, butchered her husband and her father-in-law, and if he marries Anne, he'll be half a step nearer to the throne. So he dissembles, starts to woo her."

"Dubbie, let's get the hell out of here . . . with mom and little Marvin."

But we couldn't move. The sultan held us in place. He started to rock the table like some mad, humpbacked king.

And I believed in the force of his passion. He was preparing to undertake the death of all the world. And I didn't want it to start with Dubbie, Faigele, Marvin, and me.

"Baby," he said, looking into my eyes, and I'd lost the art I picked up at Darcy's gambling den. I had to look down.

"Baby, I'm still in Manchuria . . . in that bamboo cage. Me and Skinny never got away."

He kicked over that long table. The food came tumbling down. Bottles of celery tonic crashed with all the surprise of a symphony. I managed to pull my cousin out of the way.

We got to the door.

The dark lady looked at us. "Isn't that Farouk, the cafeteria man?"

"Mom," I said, "he's insane."

"Some party. Was he planning dessert? Where's your clarinet?"

"Mom, mom, I left it with Mrs. Green."

"Yes, the wonderful Mrs. Green from the Grand Concourse . . . did she come across town to attend the party?"

Faigele didn't seize me by the ear and shove me out of the cafeteria. She left with little Marve. And Dubbie and I followed her from the darkness of the Chesterfield to the darkness under the el.

MILADY

Harve and Baby at the end of World War II.

It wasn't the party that undid me, Farouk's mad dream of Richard the Third. It wasn't the clarinet, or my Feuerman suit, or the unreliable rages of three underground men. It wasn't a letter from P.S. 61 that I happened to miss. It wasn't a truant officer who slyly appeared while I was watching *All the King's Men* at the Luxor or making my rounds as a bagman for Farouk. It was Mr. Burrell, our principal at P.S. 61. He must have examined the letters I wrote to school, over dad's signature. He wasn't thinking forgery when he took time off from his chores to visit Faigele and ask about the sick son who'd gone to a brain surgeon.

"What brain surgeon?"

He showed the letters to mom.

"Mrs. Charyn, the boy hasn't been to school in months. And if he forged those letters, my hands are tied. I have to put him on probation."

Of course I got slapped. Sergeant Sam dragged me across our apartment. What bothered him the most was that he'd accepted the "gift" of a clarinet from P.S. 61, a clarinet I couldn't even play. "My musician," he muttered.

"Dad, dad, it's a worthless piece of junk."

He slapped me again.

Marve watched with all the wisdom of a two-year-old. He was shaking. And in his terror he started to speak. "Da-da, don't hurt Jerome."

That was music, not the Board of Ed's magic ocarina. Marve must have skipped the gurgling stage. He didn't fashion little beads of language, didn't build up to one lousy word. He sang a whole sentence like some diva. We were mystified. He must have been playing on his own internal clarinet while I was at the Luxor with my briefcase. And he saved me from a terrific beating.

I had to go back to school and those clarinet lessons. But I was like a little convict at P.S. 61. My teacher, Mrs. Mahler, had to sign my name in a black book and give me a special report card, tracking my movement from hour to hour, like a leopard in a classroom cage. But I wasn't much of a leopard to the kids in my class. They were still merciless about my big ears. They flapped their arms and giggled at Dumbo, the flying elephant. Mrs. Mahler shouted at them, but she couldn't conduct a class *and* constantly shield me.

How could I fight back? I was on probation. And on

Monday mornings I had to meet with Miss de Winter, my probation officer from the Board of Ed, who would make her rounds from school to school and supervise little bandits like me. I'd never had a probation officer, and I wasn't sure what crimes she expected me to commit. I didn't even know how to masturbate.

She was important enough to occupy the principal's seat. Who the hell was Miss de Winter that she could chase Mr. Burrell out of his office? She didn't wear pants, but she had a woman's suit and tie that could have come from Feuerman & Marx. She puffed on a cigarette inside a long silver tube. She was blond as Lana Turner in *The Three Musketeers*. And I had to smile at my probation officer, because Lana Turner was D'Artagnan's foe, Lady de Winter, who had a fleur-de-lis branded into her shoulder, the mark of a common criminal. And I adored Lady de Winter, "the essence of evil," who murders the Duke of Buckingham, England's prime minister, and was the favorite spy of Cardinal Richelieu. Lady de Winter had a mole, a beauty mark, that could float across her face. She was actually the fallen wife of Athos, one of the Three Musketeers. And when the executioner arrives to lop off her head, I shivered for Lady de Winter, wanted to hold her in my arms.

I felt the same propriety about that other de Winter, my probation officer with the silver tube in her mouth. I'd been lucky, said Mr. Burrell. Most of the officers were men, who liked to bully kids on probation, ask them about their secret sexual lives. But Miss de Winter was an aristocrat. She didn't have to "feed a family" with whatever she got from the Board of Ed.

"Then why is she working in the Bronx, Mr. Burrell?"

"That's her mission," he said. "She's devoted herself to difficult cases."

I was almost giddy. I'd woken Milady's interest. That's what everybody called Lana Turner in *The Three Musketeers*. Milady.

I sat with her in Mr. Burrell's office. He'd prepared a complete dossier. I felt like someone who ought to have his own fleur-de-lis.

She read the dossier, didn't speak. Cigarette ashes fell from that silver tube.

"It's a waste of time, isn't it?"

"What?" I asked.

"School."

I wished I could find a couple more aristocrats like her.

"Spelling bees and nonsense like that. What have you been doing on your own?"

"Movies, Milady."

She smiled.

"Lady de Winter," I mumbled. "Cardinal Richelieu's pal . . . Lana Turner. The Three Musketeers."

"Am I your Milady?"

I couldn't answer her.

"Am I?"

"Yes."

"That's enough for one morning."

And she sent me back into the lions' den, where I had to endure the insults of my classmates. I couldn't stop dreaming of Miss de Winter. It didn't seem fair. We'd started a conversation, and then we had to stop. I'd have to suffer a whole week before I met her again. I resumed my lessons on the clarinet. The other kids seemed to have progressed. They could orchestrate that plastic monster by plugging and unplugging the finger holes while they blew. They'd gone from "God Bless America" to bits of Beethoven. They'd managed to conquer the beast. I was the laggard, the musical dunce.

"Dumbo shouldn't be with us," said Diana W., the prodigy of P.S. 61.

But they couldn't kick out a kid on probation.

I hadn't joined any of the cliques, wasn't invited to any of the dances that seemed so important in the school's social register. I wasn't like Henry Weintraub, king of the fox-trot, the most popular boy in our class. He had five or six girlfriends. I had a top, the digger that I kept in my pants. It took a certain finesse to make it spin. You had to twirl your wrist, and drive the digger's sharp tooth into the concrete or tar with a rapid, forceful stroke, or the digger would collapse. But the right twirl would get the digger to spin longer and much faster than an ordinary top, which only touched the surface and never "ate" into the tar. I could operate that digger with my eyes closed. But not even the most sensational spin ever put me in Henry Weintraub's league. I wasn't a fox-trotter. I was a lone boy with a top.

But I still had my wages, the wrinkled five-dollar bills I'd collected from Farouk. And I could translate that simple treasure into carfare that delivered me to the Luxor on the crosstown bus. I couldn't watch an entire film, but even half of *The Heiress* or *White Heat* was better than nothing. The Luxor was still my home, though Samson, Luke, and Murray had removed themselves from me.

I waited like a hungry little dog for my next "date" with Miss de Winter. But no matter how hard I wished, Monday wouldn't come. I blew empty air into my clarinet, triumphed with my top, and had a particular brainstorm. I visited Engine 42.

"Dan O'Brien, please," I told the house watchman.

And Dan remembered me. He brought me into the inner sanctum of a fire station, the second floor. I didn't have to hunker up the fireman's pole. We climbed a set of stairs hidden behind the trucks. I saw cots, a little stove, sleeping firemen. I didn't mention Murray. I'd come on my own.

I had baked beans with Dan, prepared on the stove. I had hot cider. He gave me my own mug, with ENGINE 42 stamped on it.

"We'll keep it here," he said. "You can always come and have a drink. The watchman will let you in."

"Am I the company mascot?"

His blue eyes didn't waver. "You're my friend."

And my session with Milady seemed a little closer. A digger meant nothing. I needed Dan O'Brien.

I had my Monday.

I rushed to the principal's office. I noticed a tiny scar under Milady's lip. I was so deeply in love with her, I would have done anything she asked. Undressed. Climbed out the window. Played pirouettes on my clarinet.

She wore a bit of powder under her left eye.

"It's a shiner," she said. "One of the boys I work with walloped me."

"Why?"

"Because I asked him too many questions."

"Will they send him to reform school?"

"He's already in reform school. I'm trying to get him out."

"Was he a hooky player, like me?"

"He didn't have to play hooky. He robbed pencils, nickels, and dimes from every boy and girl in his class. He stole sweaters and mittens and scarves."

"Was he pathological?" I asked. That was a word Dubbie had taught me. It described a Bronx disease, the loneliness of living in an archipelago, an isolation that turned you inward, got you to perform crazy deeds. "Was he pathological?"

"Not at all. It's winter. He was cold. The mittens and the money warmed him up."

"Am I pathological?"

"A little, I suppose. But we'll fix that."

"How?"

"By making you happy."

"But I am happy . . . when I'm with you."

I'd angered her. "I'm not a poodle. I'm your probation officer."

"But I'm in love with you, Milady."

She reached across the desk, grabbed my school tie, started to choke me, then changed her mind. "I'm around such violent people, I get violent. It's an occupational hazard. I'm sorry. But I'm not Lana Turner. And I'm not Milady."

"But you are Miss de Winter. And it comes to the same thing."

"Then call me Constance. You love movies. Didn't you tell me that last week?"

"I lived at a movie house when I stopped going to school. I didn't sleep there. But it's my home."

"It's an auditorium," she said. "It canvasses dreams in the dark. But you can't grow up in a movie house. And Milady can't come down from the screen."

"But she did come down."

"Charyn," she said, "shall I choke you again?"

And this time she started to laugh. She breathed into my face. I could smell the alcohol. She must have been like my dad, who could only relax with a little schnapps.

I couldn't hold onto my hour with Constance de Winter. It flew right out of my fist. And I'd fall into a black mood soon as I left the principal's office.

I rode to Monroe Avenue and Engine 42, but I had a big surprise. Dan O'Brien's pregnant wife was inside the fire station, screaming at him. "Good for nothing . . . lazy bones."

The other firemen winked and whispered to me. "A terrible shame, a terrible shame. Poor Danny-O."

"I heard that," she said. And she tossed my drinking mug at Dan. It clanked against his skull, and his eyes closed for an instant, but she couldn't have really brained him. He caught the mug as it rebounded off his head, and did his own little fireman's dance, soon as his wife ran out of the station.

"Jesus, why do you take that, Danny-O?" asked one of the firemen. "We won't have a henpecked husband in our crew."

"She's big with child," said Dan, who wasn't suffering from the blow on his head. "And the baby eats up half her blood. It gets her wild."

"Well, keep her away from the house when she's having her fits . . . or we'll replace you with Jerome."

We drank hot cider, and they sang raucous songs. I knew I couldn't live in a firehouse, but I preferred the merriment of their company to the somber tones of the cellar rats.

I was watching *White Heat* on a winter afternoon, thinking of poor Cody Jarrett (James Cagney) as a gangster who has terrible headaches and can't live without his mom, when Samson came to me, not as a conqueror ready to pull my hair and drag me into the cave, but as a supplicant, with sadness in his eyes.

"Ev, what's wrong?" I whispered in that empty movie house.

"It's Mur. I can't control him. He's gone to the fire station . . . in drag."

"Drag?"

"Dressed as Delilah."

"They'll kill him."

"I know. But he said he couldn't keep lying to his sweetheart."

"What sweetheart? Dan O'Brien has a wife. She's pregnant."

The same old anger popped into Samson's eyes. He grabbed my shirt with one of his paws. "Have you been getting chummy with Fireman Dan and Engine Forty-two?"

"Didn't you lock me out of the cellar?"

"Because you're an ambitious little brat. You hooked yourself up with King Farouk and forgot your old friends. But we don't have time to argue."

We left the Luxor and hopped into the Nash. It was starting to snow, and I marveled at the fineness of the flakes. There was no soot in the air. A thin white powder covered the streets. The Bronx had become a magic village all of a sudden, not some borderland.

Samson drove like the devil around the rim of Claremont Park. We got to the firehouse. Luke stood in the
snow, pleading with Murray Bell while Murray danced. He
was Hedy Lamarr.

"Ev," Luke said, "can't you stop this fiasco? Capture
him, for God's sake."

Delilah continued to dance. "I'll maim myself, bite off
my wrist if you come near me."

The great red door of Engine 42 opened with a rattle
that displaced bits of snow. Four firemen marched out in
their long rubber coats. They smiled at me.

"Hi, Jerome."

Before I could answer, Delilah started to sing. "Where
are you, my beloved Dan?"

The firemen shoved Luke out of the way. The tallest
one said, "What have we here? A Martian?"

"Looks like a man in woman's clothes."

"A queen," the tall fireman said, "in front of Forty-two."

"I want my Dan," Delilah cried.

"Is he trying to tell us that Danny-O has another wife?
A male bride into the bargain? That won't do."

He socked Delilah, bloodied his mouth with a single
blow. Delilah bounced on his ass. The other three firemen
plucked at him, pulled off his wig, and Delilah sat in the
snow like a bald temptress.

I waited for Samson to charge. But he didn't.

"Ev, aren't you gonna help Mur?"

"Can't. There are four of them."

"But you have Luke and me."

"I already told you. Luke's an invalid. He could drop dead from the least exertion. He has a hole in his heart."

The firemen were kicking Delilah.

"He's harmless," I said. "Leave him alone."

The tall one turned to me. His name was Milton Kell. "Jesus, I'm disappointed in you, Jerome. I thought you were one of us, our straight little man. And you travel around with a bunch of twisted people."

Kell kicked Delilah again and again.

"Don't do that."

It was Dan O'Brien, who appeared in blood-red suspenders and his blue T-shirt.

"Danny-O, are you defending these Sodomites?"

"He's a sick man, Milt. I rescued him and his mates from that burning box near the Concourse. You were there. And if you weren't so damn blind, you'd have noticed that he's been following us to all the fires. He has a craziness, that's all, a crush on me. It's nothing serious."

"Nothing serious? It's a shameful sin."

"He hasn't harmed anyone."

"What about our reputation? Doing a seductive number outside Forty-two. We'll be laughed at. They'll call us Sodom and Gomorrah. Now will you do us the honor of giving him your best kick."

"No."

Dan stepped between Delilah and the firemen, picked

Delilah up, carried him in his arms. But the tall fireman crept in front of Dan.

"You'll have to bump me out of the way. Else you're not a man."

"Bump you? You saved my skin."

"That's immaterial."

And Milton Kell clutched Delilah's clothes, tried to strip him, create his own burlesque on Monroe Avenue. Dan had to put Murray down. Then he began to fight the tall fireman. I wanted to close my eyes, but I couldn't. It was like a swift and brutal ballet. Only a pair of punches were traded. Dan's fists hardly flew. But the tall fireman crumpled to the sidewalk with a swollen eye and fell asleep. Dan picked up Delilah again, continued his journey to Samson's car. He dropped Delilah into the back of the Nash.

"Thank you, thank you, for beating up that bully," Samson said.

"That bully's my best friend. Now will you drive away from here and don't ever come back . . . including Jerome."

I pleaded with Dan. "It's not my fault. I didn't ask Murray to dance."

"Don't come back."

I mourned my drinking mug and the gentleness of Dan and my mates at Engine 42, even if they'd almost crippled

Delilah. All I had were those three scoundrels. They invited me back into their cave. I smoked Fatimas with them. Delilah was so forlorn, he wouldn't speak.

I told the three of them about my own fatal passion.

"I'm in love with my probation officer."

I'd piqued Delilah's interest. His mouth was twitching. "Does he have big biceps?"

"It's not a he. Her name's Miss de Winter."

Delilah fell back into silence, and Samson mocked me. "That's ridiculous ... I suppose you'll marry her when you're eighteen."

"I might," I said. "I might."

I had to feed off my own blood until Monday. Met Miss de Winter with my heart in my mouth.

"Stop ogling me," she said. "It's indecent."

"Constance, you're the last friend I have in the world. No one invites me to a single dance. I'm an outlaw. They call me Dumbo in class. They laugh at me during music lessons."

She sucked on her long cigarette holder. "I could punish your class, but it's hopeless, isn't it? Let's get the hell out of here."

Miss de Winter had her own mandate, and it was more powerful than Mr. Burrell's. He couldn't prevent me from leaving P.S. 61 at ten in the morning. It was like playing hooky with a stamp of approval from the Board of Ed.

"Would you like art or animals?" she asked.

"I don't understand."

"A museum or the Bronx Zoo?"

"Animals," I said.

We took a trolley along the spine of Dubbie's archipelago and arrived at Bronx Park. We looked for the lions behind the enormous ditch of the Bronx's own "African Plains," but lions were scarce in the winter.

"Constance, were you ever married?"

"Twice."

"What happened?"

"I couldn't last very long with any man. I'm a jungle creature."

"But lions and tigers marry. They never leave their mates. That's what Mrs. Mahler says."

"Then I'm an unlucky lioness. And stop asking questions."

We had lunch in the zoo's cafeteria. Her hands were shaking. I had to light her cigarette. She drank from a flask that she pulled out of her shoulder bag. I was already mourning her. I knew she wouldn't last as my probation officer.

"Constance, will I ever see you again?"

"Silly," she said, "have I missed a Monday appointment with you?"

But I'd educated myself at the Luxor and other movie houses. I could read faces on the screen, and Constance had all the dark dimensions of a movie face. Perhaps she wasn't Lana Turner's double, but she was a dark lady with blond hair . . . and a fleur-de-lis. An executioner was waiting for her *somewhere*.

"I'll never graduate," I said.

"You will."

"They'll put me in reform school . . . or worse."

"If you're going to snivel I'll slap your face."

"You're an officer. You can't slap a kid."

"Didn't I almost strangle you?"

"That was different," I said. "I was flirting with you."

"And what are you doing now?"

"Declaring my love."

"Because I remind you of Lana Turner."

"You're beautiful, and you'll always be my Lady de Winter, but Constance, it's more than that. You're the one school officer who can ever admit that school is a big fat lie."

"And what will you do, my darling musketeer? Deliver groceries?"

"I don't care."

She kissed her own hand and then touched my cheek with it. I had to hug myself to keep from falling. How else could I deal with that delicious shock? A kiss imprinted on her hand. She hailed a taxicab, drove me to my block.

"Out, out," she said. I could feel her affection. She waved to me, but I didn't wave back.

I dreaded the week to come. I'd have blue Mondays for the rest of my life. The Luxor was my last outpost. I sat in the cave with Samson and Delilah. Delilah had turned catatonic. He stared at the walls.

"Where's Luke?"

"With Mrs. Green," Samson said. "Would you like to meet her? You're not a hooky player any more. She can't harm you."

But I wasn't in the mood to meet Everett and Luke's strange companion. I couldn't discuss Constance with her. She might have tattled to the Board of Ed.

"I'll meet her another time."

"We told her about you, Baby. She wants to be your friend."

On Wednesday, after class, I returned to the cave with my clarinet. The rats weren't around. An enormous woman with an orange wig sat in their place like some Lady Goliath. Her shoulders and arms and stooped carriage seemed slightly familiar.

"Hello, Baby," she said in a hoarse voice. "Would you mind if I kissed you? You're a handsome boy."

I stood on my toes and walloped her with all my might. She didn't seem to mind. I walloped her again and pulled off her wig. It was Everett. Delilah must have come out of her melancholy for a minute and coached him how to play a woman.

"There is no Mrs. Green," I said. "You made it all up."

"I did not. I wouldn't lie to you, Baby. She got sick of Luke and me, left us flat."

"And you put on an orange wig."

"I can't help myself."

I slapped his face. He smiled.

"You wouldn't even protect Murray from those firemen. You're a mouse. You would have let Mur get killed. Dan O'Brien had to fight his own mates. It was our battle, not his."

"But I took you into our club, let you have free seats at the Luxor . . ."

"So you could ask me for a kiss."

His shoulders started to heave. I'd never heard a man cry so hard. But I couldn't forgive him. I walked out of the Luxor with all the dread of a boy who'd lost his home.

I sat in the principal's office Monday morning and waited for a woman I knew would never come. It was Mr. Burrell who showed up, like a kind shadow of doom.

"My probation officer isn't coming back, is she, Mr. Burrell?"

"I think not," he said, like some character out of King Farouk's favorite play. "But it isn't all bad news, Jerome. I'm taking you off probation."

"Why?"

He seemed startled, as if a snake had bitten him.

"I'm not ready, Mr. Burrell. I need Miss de Winter."

"But she's the one who recommended it . . . before she resigned."

"She promised to be here. Did she leave any messages for me?"

He must have seen the starkness in my face, the terror that unrequited love can bring.

"She's a sick woman, Jerome. Very sick."

"She in the hospital, Mr. Burrell? Is that why she had to skip her Monday appointments?"

"I told you. She resigned."

"Can you give me her address?"

"That's impossible," he said. "We never reveal the personal addresses of our probation officers. It would leave them vulnerable to some madman's attack."

"I'm not a madman," I said.

"Jerome, you'll have to return to your class."

It was like a nightmare at 11:00 A.M. Not even Mrs. Mahler could stop all the snickering, and she tried. I was big for my age and I would have fought it out with Henry Weintraub, man to man. But he wouldn't fight me, wouldn't fox-trot with his fists. My classmates had scratched "Dumbo" all over my desk. We were studying the rules of grammar, but I wanted to break the rules. Neither mom nor dad could write. Harvey had been the scholar of the house. But he was far away, and I was the one who had to write complete sentences to the landlord and the grocer (about an unpaid bill). And I longed to write incomplete sentences, filled with the wildest grammar. . . .

I returned home for lunch. But I couldn't eat. After a

day or two, mom left Marvin in his stroller long enough to start noticing me.

"You're skinny like a chicken. What's wrong?"

"Mom, my probation officer disappeared."

"Good. We'll go to the Roxy and celebrate."

The Roxy was Manhattan's most splendid movie palace. And on my birthday Faigele kept to a rigid pattern: she'd prepare a chocolate cake which only I was allowed to slice and then we'd ride downtown to the Roxy, catch the stage show and a film like *The Farmer's Daughter*, with Loretta Young as a Swedish servant girl who decides to run for Congress. That was our slice of America. But I didn't want America. I wanted Milady.

"Mom, there's nothing to celebrate . . . Miss de Winter was nice to me. She's sick. And Mr. Burrell won't let me have her address."

"You can't interfere in her private life."

"But we were friends. She wouldn't run away like that . . . without a message."

"It's not a telegraph service, your school. She doesn't have to leave messages to every boy on probation."

I returned to school. I dreamed at my desk, had forebodings about the executioner in *The Three Musketeers* who lops off Milady's head. In my dreams I suddenly saw behind the executioner's mask. The executioner was me. Somehow I'd been elected to kill Constance. I was the culprit who'd kept her away from P.S. 61.

I skipped the clarinet lesson. I'd never master that crazy

kazoo. I was banished from Engine 42 on account of Delilah, and I couldn't go back to the Luxor and pretend that
Samson hadn't put on an orange wig to steal a kiss from
me. I went to the cafeteria. I had money in my pocket. I
was King Farouk's little bagman. I ordered a celery tonic.
I wanted to discuss Corregidor with the caid, because I had
a feeling that I'd started my own death march, without the
benefit of Japanese bayonets. But I couldn't find Farouk.
He wasn't at his table. And neither was his bodyguard, Tyrone. With all its girth and its endless counter, the cafeteria
seemed like some shallow place without a proper king.
There wasn't much mystery or romance.

I starved for a week. Dad locked me in the closet. I
didn't panic. I could see Constance much clearer in the
dark. And finally mom decided to visit Mr. Burrell. She'd
wheel Marve to school in his stroller.

"Mom," I said, "the kids will make fun of me . . . my
own mother has to bail me out."

"Then stop the hunger strike."

"How? I lost my appetite."

She went to school with Marve and her silver fox coat.
Dealing for the dentist must have taught her the art of
politics. And perhaps beauty has its own persuasion. I'm
not sure. But she got Miss de Winter's address from Mr.
Burrell.

"Faigele," I said, "you're a magician."

"It's a lie. I'm a greenhorn in a fur coat that will soon
be bald."

"A greenhorn who dealt cards at the Concourse Plaza and took on the whole Democratic Party."

Mom was about to cry. "And deserted our only god, Franklin Roosevelt."

"Didn't he desert Darcy? You had to be loyal to the dentist, mom. But how did you wheedle that address from Burrell?"

"I didn't wheedle. I begged. I told him it would look bad in the school's records if he had a dying boy on his hands."

"Did you smile at him, mom?"

The dark lady shook her head. "Maybe once or twice."

I was hoping Faigele might run for Congress, like the farmer's daughter. But she would have had to study grammar with me at P.S. 61, and what would happen to little Marve?

We went downtown on the Third Avenue el, mom, Marve, me, and the stroller, and arrived in the empire of Manhattan, which had nothing to do with our own archipelago. We had the Concourse, yes, and the Bronx Zoo, but they were only little outposts. We were on Millionaires' Mile, between Madison and Park, which housed *half* the nation's wealth. The Concourse may have had a couple of millionaires, but it couldn't match the panoramic sweep of tall apartment palaces. I was dizzy and lost and overwhelmed. I wanted to return to our terrain, hike in one of the dunes . . . or enjoy the darkness of another Luxor. But there were no other Luxors in the Bronx. And

I had to meet Milady again . . . even if she lived on Park Avenue.

Mom introduced us to the doorman. I had to count on all her wiles. He was already in her spell when she pronounced, "De Winter, please."

"Old Mrs. de Winter or young, ma'am?"

"Both," mom said.

The doorman muttered into the intercom, savoring mom with his eyes. Then he winked at all of us, including Marve.

"Mrs. de Winter will see you, ma'am."

He signaled to the elevator man, who sat on a tall chair and drove us up into the interior sky of that particular palace. We stopped on the twenty-first floor. Faigele seemed very nervous. I watched her look in the mirror of the gold-rimmed elevator car. She didn't have to paint her lips. She was the dark lady from Belorusse who touched the bits of gray in her hair.

The elevator man offered little Marve a lollipop. He couldn't take his eyes off Faigele. He pointed to a door that was dark blue. Faigele didn't have to knock or ring a bell. The door opened, and a tall woman who was much, much grayer than mom let us all in. Old Mrs. de Winter. She could have been ninety. How could I tell? But her back wasn't bent, and she walked with the grace of a ballerina (I'd seen *Red Shoes* at the Roxy, about a ballerina who dances herself to death). Still, she didn't have the ripeness of Milady.

Mrs. de Winter asked us into the living room, which was two stories high, had enormous picture windows that peered over the rooftops and revealed the pastures of Central Park.

She served us little cakes, invited us to share a pot of tea. I didn't want to be impolite, but I hadn't come to Park Avenue for cake and tea.

"Mrs. de Winter," I said, "is Constance here?"

"Yes, child. But I'm afraid you can't see her."

"I wouldn't dream of bothering her, but we had a date at P.S. Sixty-one."

"That's the problem," said Mrs. de Winter. "She had too many dates."

Faigele touched my hand: it was a language we'd developed when mom had been a dealer. I was supposed to shut up and let the dark lady do the talking.

"You see," Mrs. de Winter said, "my daughter has absorbed the pain of all the children in her charge. It was too much for her. She can't deliver the whole public school system, and she wouldn't work at a private school, which would have been a safety net."

"She wasn't looking for safety nets," mom said. "She prefers children like my Jerome."

"She's had a breakdown, Mrs. Charyn. Frankly, she tried to kill herself."

"I'm so sorry, Mrs. de Winter. . . . Baby, we'd better go."

Faigele stood up. And Mrs. de Winter seemed uncertain all of a sudden.

"Have I disappointed your son, Mrs. Charyn?"

"He doesn't eat," mom said. "But it's his fault . . . he shouldn't have attached himself to his probation officer. He's eleven years old and he's in love. But he'll recover."

We started to leave. Mom pushed the stroller. Mrs. de Winter rocked on her heels, like the ballerina in *Red Shoes*.

"Would it help, Mrs. Charyn, if your Jerome could see Constance one last time? Then she wouldn't have broken her date . . . but he'll have to promise to eat again."

"I promise."

And old Mrs. de Winter brought our little tribe into Milady's room. I was shivering. The woman I loved wanted to die. She was reading a book in bed. Both her wrists were bandaged. She wore pajamas and a red robe. I thought of Cardinal Richelieu, who was always in red.

Constance's book was called *The Heart Is a Lonely Hunter*. I didn't understand the title. How could any heart hunt? Constance didn't even smile when she saw me. But she smiled at little Marve. And she was very curious about the dark lady.

"Constance," Mrs. de Winter said, "this is Jerome's mother, Mrs. Charyn, and his baby brother."

"I know," Milady said. "Mother, you've made the introduction. You can leave now. They won't bite."

"But you're tired, dear. I'll allow them ten minutes."

"Fifteen," Milady said. "A conversation can't kill me."

Constance was much more animated once Mrs. de Winter had left the room. She found her silver tube, plugged a cigarette into one end, and started to puff. She wouldn't even look at me.

"Would you like a cigarette, Mrs. Charyn?"

"Call me Faigele, please."

And the two dark ladies were smoking together, like accomplices.

"Faigele, I wish I could have helped Jerome. But I can't. His imagination is much too big for a classroom . . . and what about you?" Constance asked Marve.

"I don't have imagination," Marve said. "I'm too young for school."

Mom and Marve sat on Milady's bed. They were having a terrific time. I was locked out of their little trinity. I understood that title now. My heart was the loneliest hunter in Manhattan.

Milady kissed Marve. He and mom said good-bye. I started to leave with them, and that's when Constance looked into my eyes. "You," she said, "you stay."

And soon I was all alone with her.

"I'll slap you if you cry."

"But I can't bear those bandages on your wrists."

"Don't pity me," she said.

"Milady . . ."

"I don't want your declarations of love. I missed my appointment. I let you down. I'm trying to make it up. But don't you ever come here again. Your mother can come, not you."

"Milady . . ."

"I'm not a healer, do you understand?"

"Milady . . ."

"Swear to me that you won't quit school."

"Milady, I can't live without you."

"Swindler," she said, "you learned that talk at the movies. I won't have RKO and MGM inside my bedroom, you hear?"

"Yes, Milady."

"And if you don't graduate from P.S. Sixty-one and go to junior high, I'll become a harpy and haunt every dream you have."

"I wouldn't mind."

She laughed and bit into that silver tube. "Get out of here."

I walked out of the bedroom, but I wouldn't say goodbye, or admit to myself that I couldn't see Constance again. I'd grow as rich as the Great Gatsby, and Constance would have to take me in.

STANISLAUS

Dubbie and the dark lady with two of my uncles, c. 1947.

n spite of my losses, I still had a Feuerman suit, kept in a closet at the cafeteria. But the caid forgot to give me a key. And how would I ever win Constance back if I couldn't dress to kill? The Chesterfield was like a funeral parlor without Farouk. I sat in a corner and sipped celery tonic . . . until Tyrone appeared. He had a demon in his eye.

"Been looking all over for you, Jerome."

"And I've been looking for Farouk."

"Don't get sassy, little man. We have to find your cousin."

"Which cousin?" I asked.

And the king's bodyguard slapped me right off my chair. The Chesterfield lost whatever breath it had. We were swimming in silence, me and Tyrone. The countermen stared at us. Tyrone drank a bit of celery tonic. There were ripples of anger in his cheeks. The taste of celery must have pleased him, because the rippling stopped.

"Tyrone," I said from the cafeteria's floor, my face still tingling from the slap. "I thought you can't stand celery soda."

The bodyguard bowed to me. "I can't. But whenever I'm anxious I make an exception."

He scooped me back into my seat and bowed again. "I apologize. And let me repeat. We have to find your cousin with the curly hair . . . the whiz."

"Dubbie Yellin."

"That's right. The girl who can recite Shakespeare."

"But why's she so important?"

"The king's gone out of his mind. And only the sound of Shakespeare can soothe him . . . come on."

Tyrone started to drag me along. "What about my Feuerman suit? Shouldn't I wear it if we're meeting the king?"

"This is an emergency. The suit can sit and wait."

We got into Tyrone's black sedan and rode across the Bronx River to Dubbie's high school. The bodyguard was impatient. He wanted to pull my cousin out of her classroom.

"That would be great," I said. "Kidnapping a student."

"I don't care. I told you. It's an emergency."

"But Dubbie will care. You'll humiliate her in front of her mates. And she might not be so kind to the king."

We sat for half an hour. The school began to empty out. There wasn't a single black face.

"It's marshmallow land," Tyrone said. "The righteous and the rich."

"Dubbie's not rich. And it's not her fault if colored people can't cross the Bronx River and attend James Monroe."

"Then whose fault is it, my little man?"

"Congress, I guess. Or the City Council. Or our borough president, Fred R. Lions."

"Or the whole goddamn white nation. But I don't have time to argue. Your cousin must have gone off somewhere with the basketball team. You'll have to play her part."

"Tyrone," I said. "I'm not a girl."

"But you'll have to pretend you are and talk Shakespeare to the king. Richard the Third and all that razzmatazz."

I continued my lament. "We don't study Shakespeare in the sixth grade."

"Tough."

"How can I remember the lines of a humpbacked king I never met?"

"Use your imagination, little man. Make it up."

We rode back to *our* side of the Bronx River with all the force of a fire truck. The cops didn't chase after us. Tyrone must have had some special immunity. But there was a much greater riddle. Where could Farouk be if he wasn't at the cafeteria? He slept in the back room and lived in his own corner, where daylight couldn't reach him and corrupt his skin with the least bit of sunshine. We galloped across the Bronx, and I began to get suspicious. I wondered if Farouk's whole life was a big fat fairy tale.

We parked near Addie Vallin's, the prima donna of ice-cream parlors, located between Yankee Stadium and the Concourse Plaza. It was a legendary spot, like Radio City Music Hall. But Radio City didn't have a picture of Babe Ruth on the wall, wolfing down ten chocolate sundaes at a time. Judges ate at Addie Vallin's. Joe DiMaggio had his own private booth, because unlike the Babe, DiMaggio loved to eat alone. Fred Lions conducted half his deals at Addie Vallin's. And it was the dentist's favorite watering hole. Darcy had ruled Addie Vallin's during the war. He would dance into the ice cream parlor after a poker game, with me and mom, and all the soda jerks would salute their own prince, who kept Republican politicians and local hoods out of Addie Vallin's, because he had his own muscle. Police captains, judges, party chiefs, and Democratic ward heelers were all beholden to Darce. And Addie Vallin's was where he'd dispense cash to the party faithful. I'd watch him toss a thick envelope to a captain or a judge, while he spooned ice cream into his mouth and winked at the dark lady. Ah, I thought to myself, like a little champion who'd been kicked out of paradise. Ah, those were the days . . .

I didn't see the sultan. He wasn't at the counter or at any of the booths. I studied the celebrities on the walls. The Babe. Joltin' Joe. John Garfield, who'd been a juvenile delinquent long before he was a movie star. He'd played a Jewish boxer in *Body and Soul* and a fiddler from the streets in *Humoresque*, and that's why every male child, including me, wanted to become a boxer or a virtuoso on the violin, like Johnny G. It didn't matter that Garfield ended badly in both films, that he'd sacrificed his own guts to the gods of success. We'd have danced with the devil to have a bit of *Body and Soul*.

Tyrone found his king. Farouk was hiding near the toilets. He had his own little niche behind the last booth, at a table that was much too small for him. His flesh seemed to spill onto the tabletop. He was stuffing balls of ice cream into his mouth with his own fat fists. He couldn't stop eating. Tyrone had to grab Farouk's ice-cream bowl away from him.

"You're signing your own death warrant," Farouk grumbled.

"It won't be the first time," said Tyrone, who wiped the king's lips, cheeks, and hands with one of Addie Vallin's huge napkins. I'd never seen so much tenderness in a man. Tyrone must have loved the Bronx's mad Egyptian in his own mysterious way.

"Where's that Dubbie Yellin, the little daughter who talks like Lady Anne?"

"I couldn't grab her," Tyrone said. "She wasn't at her high school. But I could steal a professor from Fordham, a Shakespeare specialist."

"I don't want a prof. That's not Shakespeare, it's only stinking scholarship. What did you bring me, Ty?"

"The little daughter's cousin. Jerome."

"That piss-in-the-pants? He works for me."

"But some of the little daughter's Shakespeare rubbed off on him."

"I don't believe it."

"You better believe it," Tyrone said. "King, we can't stay here."

"Why not?"

"This is Addie Vallin's, not some neighborhood sugar bowl. Meyer Lansky could come in any minute. The Little Man hates Manhattan ice cream. He rides uptown every afternoon for a black and tan."

A black and tan was a coffee ice-cream soda laced with chocolate sauce. It was invented at Addie Vallin's. And that's why the soda jerks at Addie were treated like maestros and never had to worry about a minimum wage. Customers spoiled them rotten with tips, and their salary doubled that of any other soda jerk.

"Meyer," Farouk said, mocking his bodyguard. "What's Meyer compared to Richard?"

"Sultan," I said, "aren't they both murderers and maniacs?"

Farouk didn't even bother to look at me. That's how low I was in his esteem. "Meyer's a pistolero who made it big. He has a thousand pairs of white underpants. They're all spotless. That's America for you. The man in white underpants. But he never had a bump on his back. Did dogs ever bark at the Little Man? Was his shadow bent, like Richard's? Could he ever have dared say, 'My kingdom for a horse'?"

"Sultan, what would a horse do in Addie Vallin's?"

"Eat ice cream, you imbecile," Farouk said, with such narrowness in his eyes, I would have preferred to disappear.

"Meyer's a horse," Tyrone said, "and Meyer will bite your head off."

But the sultan smiled at Tyrone. "He had his chance."

"Meyer saw you at Addie Vallin's?"

"Coming in and out of the toilet."

"Did he have his goons with him?"

"He doesn't need goons. Meyer's a street fighter. He could have broken me with his bare hands."

"And he did nothing? Let you sit and eat coffee ice cream?"

"He's generous. He paid for another dish. And he asked me about Corregidor. He wanted the details. I said, 'Mr. Lansky, a death march is a death march. There's nothing to it.' He would never hurt a Jewish war hero. That's what he said. But why did I dishonor him and the state of Israel by keeping pictures of an Egyptian king on my walls? I told him, 'Mr. Lansky, it's my cafeteria.' "

" 'Then close your cafeteria,' he said, 'or I'll close you.' But he couldn't afford to be impolite. Addie Vallin's is like royalty. If he bludgeoned me where I sat, the soda shop would banish him, and he could never have another black and tan."

"And what if his goons punish you when you're not on hallowed ground? King, we have to get away from here."

"Not while I'm blue."

"And what the hell are you blue about?"

"I can't get Baby's mother out of my mind."

"Should she leave her husband and move into the Chesterfield?"

"You could kill him for me, Ty."

I saw the anger build in Tyrone's cheeks.

"Farouk, is this Richard the Third? Because I don't remember being inside any plays. And Jerome might have a couple ideas about his dad's mortality."

Tyrone turned to me. "Don't pay attention to him. He's sick in the head."

"Where's Buckingham?" Farouk mumbled, "and all my other murderers and men for hire? I need thee not."

Tyrone nudged me. "Humor him, little man . . . just sing like a jackass. He'll think it's Shakespeare."

"Is this the good Lady Anne?"

Tyrone nudged me again, a little harder. And I jumped right into Shakespeare.

"Yes, Your Majesty."

"Madam, I'll die of want until I lie with you."

"Yes, Your Majesty."

"Could you love a man who cannot even pass before a looking glass?"

I didn't know what to say. But Tyrone was pinching my leg.

"I'll try, Your Majesty."

"Anne, what delight have I? But to see my shadow in the sun . . . and descant on mine own deformity."

"Majesty," I said, "there are worse things in life than a hunchback."

I was getting warmed up when Farouk started to cry, and Tyrone pulled the bulk of him up from the table and carried him out of Addie Vallin's and into the black Hudson. If Meyer's men were around, they didn't interfere. How could they have murdered such a pathetic king?

I went to school. I wasn't a truant. But I had no other friend or accomplice than Tyrone. I brought him to our basement on Seabury Place and introduced him to our black Super, Haines, who'd had his skull bashed in by Meyer's henchmen. Haines had to use all his willpower to shovel coal. He'd once been the Wyatt Earp of our neighborhood, protecting the weak from whatever bullies were around.

"I remember him," Tyrone said before we climbed down to the cellar. "He was famous on Boston Road . . . the nigger Super who plays sheriff for white folks."

"Don't you belittle him," I said.

But when Tyrone saw Haines shoveling bits of coal in some powerful oblivion, his own heart must have squeezed, because he rolled up the cuffs of his canary-yellow jacket and started shoveling for Haines. Then they sat on the cellar's sooty chairs and smoked Fatimas.

"Are you Baby's employer?" Haines asked.

"Not at all. We're both in bondage to a man called Farouk. I'm Tyrone Wood."

And the Super summoned up something from his own damaged memory box.

"Tyrone Wood. Wasn't you with the Boston Road Blackies? Didn't I pin your ears back once?"

"You sure did, Super. Six of us at a time. I'd never taken a whopping like that."

"Did it straighten you out?"

"No. But it humbled me. And now I go into battle with two lead pipes."

We left the Super down in the coal bins, and Tyrone had to wipe his eyes with a handkerchief.

"Ty, did you ever see Garfield in *Body and Soul*? He had to fight a colored champion named Ben, but Garfield didn't want to do it, because Ben had brain problems. He'd been—"

"That's Canada Lee. He was a real boxer before he went to acting school. He could have knocked hell out of a hundred Garfields. But he lost an eye in the ring."

"It fell out of his head while he was fighting?"

"Yeah. In the middle of the third round. He would have kept battling, but the referee stopped the fight."

"That's just like the Super. He finished off the goons that crowned him and cracked his skull."

"Keep quiet," Tyrone said, and put away his handker-chief. We'd gotten my Feuerman suit out of Farouk's closet. I had my homburg and my silk tie. Tyrone had managed to resettle Farouk in his old station at the Chester-field, and the cafeteria was functioning again. It had its caid. And we could visit Bronx delicatessens, take new orders for celery tonic, and collect old bills. And sometimes Tyrone would bring me to the little black enclave where he lived, south of Crotona Park. And that's when I realized that Farouk's bodyguard was the caid of Boston Road. He didn't operate out of a cafeteria. Ty's headquarters was a Baptist church. He had his own back room, where the ministers would relax and sip celery tonic that Tyrone supplied and meet with members of their congregation. But the colored caid claimed this room a couple of times a week. He would sit in an upholstered chair, like our borough president, and caucus with his own "congregation."

Men would arrive in their Sunday suits, whisper in Tyrone's ear, feed him bundles of cash, which he crammed into his pockets or gave me to count. I couldn't tell what kind of transactions were going on, but I listened with all my might, and I realized that the caid wouldn't tolerate any hustling of heroin in his streets.

"Shorty," I heard him say, "I don't care what shit you swallow or shoot into your veins, but if one schoolkid dies of an overdose, you die."

"Goddamn, that's cool with me."

"Tighten up. Don't say 'goddamn' in the Lord's house."

"Who's that little man in the chapeau and million-dollar suit?" asked Shorty, who was as big as Samson but didn't have Samson's long hair.

"My lawyer," Tyrone said. "Baby Jerome."

Shorty scrutinized me from top to toe. "Awful young to be a lawyer, Ty."

"Baby's a genius. He took the bar exams at ten."

"But no judge would let a shrimp like that argue a case."

"He doesn't have to fool around with judges. He has a private practice. I'm his only client."

"Would he give me some advice?"

"Ask him yourself. He isn't deaf and dumb."

Shorty hunkered down and practically nibbled my ear. "Counselor, I have matrimonial problems. Four wives. They all got together and are threatening to drag me into court unless I pay them a significant fee. Ty says it ain't legal if I punch 'em out and commit a little homicide on their lawyer. What the heck should I do?"

"Disappear for a while. They can't bleed an invisible man."

Shorty slapped his own knee and stuffed ten dollars into the brim of my homburg.

"Ty, he's pure silk. Would you lend the little man out to me?"

"No. He's all mine."

And this Samson marched out of Tyrone's little sacristy, singing to himself, "Can't bleed an invisible man."

But I was more interested in the women of Tyrone's congregation. I couldn't bear to look at them. They were almost as beautiful as Constance or Faigele. And Tyrone had a particular dark lady. Paula, who hovered over him in her high heels. She didn't wear lipstick or mascara in church.

"Bossman," she said, "we haven't gone dancing in two weeks."

"I've had business problems. And besides, it might not be safe to go strutting with my best little fox. Meyer Lansky has his own nigger spies. He smells money and blood. He thinks we're a hot territory. He'd like to bring his jukeboxes to Boston Road."

"But we don't have to dance in public, Ty . . . can I kiss your little man? He's got the cutest lips."

"You wanna make me jealous, girl?"

Paula started to laugh, and her whole body shivered. Suddenly I wanted to be a man, not some facsimile in a Feuerman suit.

"Where's he from?" Paula asked.

"His ma's from Russia. Baby, ain't that right?"

"Belorusse," I said.

"I thought so. He has Russian eyes."

And Paula took me in her arms and kissed me long and hard on the mouth.

"Bossman," she said. "I could drink him up."

I would have kissed her back, but how could I have been unfaithful to Tyrone with his best fox?

103

When Ty noticed a delegation of colored women near the door, he shoved Paula out of his sacristy. These women were from the Parents Association at Morris High. Their sons and daughters attended Morris, and they were chagrined.

"Tyrone Wood," the chief delegate said, "are we going to have a high school for coloreds only for the rest of our lives?"

"What can I do, Mother?"

"Agitate."

"A colored man's agitation don't mean much in the big bad world."

"Well, you're part of that world. Use your influence, Tyrone. Our children are dying of loneliness. The politicians have boxed us in. Can't they bring some white boys and girls into our district? What would it cost them?"

"Blood, I suppose. Pride. They're scared of us, Mother, scared of our skin."

"Then make them unscared, Tyrone. Or we'll march into their precious James Monroe and shut it down."

"Yes'm," Tyrone said, like a chastened child. And after the delegation was gone, he whispered to me, "Jerome, you think we could get your cousin together with the Morris Mothers? I mean, if they had a white student on their list, a student from James Monroe . . ."

"Ty," I said, "you're just like the Super, battling for people all the time."

"I am not. There's a big difference. I don't have a crack in my head and I'm not shoveling coal."

"I'll talk to Dubbie, but admit it. You're the new Wyatt Earp."

"Go on," he said. "Worship a white sheriff. But leave me out of it." And he shut his little sacristy.

I went about my business. I wore the homburg, collected for Farouk, and had black and tans with Tyrone at Addie Vallin's. The ice-cream parlor wasn't segregated. Tyrone didn't have to eat at a special booth. But I began to wonder about things. There were black ballplayers in the American League, Larry Doby and Satchel Paige of the Cleveland Indians, and I'm sure Addie Vallin's welcomed them when Cleveland came to town. Yet the Yankees themselves were snow white. I longed for a black DiMaggio, but he didn't seem to appear. And Ty told me stories about colored ballplayers who had their own big leagues, their own stars, like Josh Gibson, Judy Johnson, Cool Papa Bell . . . and Satchel Paige, who was sold to Cleveland by the Kansas City Monarchs just before he was fifty.

"I read the stats," I said. "Satchel Paige is forty-one."

"Fifty. You think the Indians would have grabbed him if he hadn't lied about his age? He's still a knuckleball artist. The white boys can't hit his junk. And DiMaggio's a child compared to Judy and Josh."

"You've seen them play? Where?" I asked greedily. "Where?"

"At Yankee Stadium . . . don't you think we have our own all-star games? But it's a colored-only clientele."

"Wouldn't the coloreds let me in?"

"If you promise to behave." And Tyrone touched his pointed little beard. "We'd have to give you a street name. That's what a Blackie uses when he's on the run."

"Why would I need it?"

"In case the cops come and start arresting people. Nigger ball isn't always legal."

"What's your street name, Ty?"

"Amanda Little."

"But that sounds like a woman."

"It's supposed to sound like a woman. It confuses the cops. Only a badass would wear a woman's name."

"But I'm not that bad. Didn't Farouk call me piss-in-the-pants?"

"How can I take piss-in-the-pants to see the next Cool Papa Bell if he doesn't have a proper tag?"

I thought and thought. But I couldn't use Faigele or Dubbie or Constance. It would have been like stealing a person's soul.

"Be quick about it. The nigger leagues are dying day by day. White baseball is starting to steal all the talent. And it's a pity. Because black baseball was like a tumbling war. It was dangerous . . . well, what's your tag?"

"Delilah," I said.

And Tyrone tried it on his tongue. "Delilah. That's chic."

"When can we go to a black baseball game?"

"Soon," he said.

And we made our usual tour of Bronx delicatessens, both of us dressed to kill. I wished Faigele could see me in my homburg hat. Her middle son was rising in the world, even if Farouk paid me peanuts. Tyrone chatted with the delicatessen owners, and I sang Delilah, Delilah, Delilah. But I was a boy with a street name who hadn't bothered to watch the street. When we came out of the fifth delicatessen, a band of white men was waiting for us. They wore homburgs, like me, and carried baseball bats.

"Baby," Tyrone said, "run."

The alarm in his eyes was for Delilah, not himself. He bowed to the white men. "Give Meyer my love," he said, and got into their Cadillac. Two of the white men ran into the deli and smashed the counter and the hot table where frankfurters sizzled, and then they attacked the counter-man, hitting him once, twice over the head. They walked out of the deli, whistling to themselves, and handed me one of the bats.

"Here, kid, a toy from your Uncle Meyer."

The bat had blood all over it.

I could see Tyrone's eyes in the depths of the Cadillac. He must have been disappointed in Delilah. I didn't run. The two white men got into the Cadillac, and the car took off like some clipper that could sail without the sea.

The cops arrived seconds after the Cadillac was gone. They could have been sitting around the corner. They called an ambulance for the counterman and seized the baseball bat.

"Quite an active little fella, aren't you? What's your name?" asked a fat cop.

"Delilah," I said.

"Delilah? That's lovely."

And the same fat cop punched me in the mouth.

"Jerome," I said. "I'm Little Charyn."

They threw me into their police car and drove me to the Forty-first Precinct on Simpson Street, which would become famous as Fort Apache when the Bronx started to burn in the '70s, but was quieter in 1949. I had my own cage, because I couldn't be locked up with adults. And why did I start dreaming of my dead dog? Beauty. I missed her all of a sudden, even if she'd never loved me and only loved mom. I was lent to a pair of bulls, Johnson and McQueen, who had big, beefy faces. They fed me a peanut butter sandwich from their canteen, took me out of the cage, and interrogated me.

"Charyn, what's this Delilah business? Are you with the Boston Road Blackies? That's brilliant of Mr. Wood. To hire a white scout. Why'd you beat up an old man and ruin his delicatessen?"

"I didn't beat him up."

"Then was it the Holy Ghost who was clutching a baseball bat?"

"It was Meyer Lansky's gang. They clobbered that old man and gave me the bat . . . I'm a salesman, that's all."

"And what do you sell?"

"Celery tonic."

Both detectives laughed. "That's a wondrous tale. Meyer's become a bootlegger, eh? He's out to steal your franchise. The baron of celery soda."

"Meyer's not interested in celery soda," I said. "He wants to get his jukeboxes into Boston Road, and the Blackies wouldn't let him. So he kidnapped Ty."

"Meyer doesn't kidnap coons. It's beneath his dignity. No, Tyrone and that crazy King Farouk were trying to force their product upon delicatessens in the East Bronx. Ty's 'convincer' was a baseball bat. He bopped the old man, and when our lads showed up, he ran away and left you with the handle."

"It's a lie," I said. "Tyrone wouldn't leave me flat."

Johnson nudged McQueen. "What do we have here? A convert to the colored cause. Line up with us, Little Charyn. It's your only chance. We'll defend you at Children's Court, sing your praises to the judge. Or you'll sit at Spofford with a bunch of satanic boys."

Spofford was like a concentration camp for children, a crime school where the baddest boys had to stay before they were sentenced. I'd have to kiss P.S. 61 good-bye. No more celery tonic, no more screenings of *Twelve O'Clock High*.

"Sign," Johnson said, "sign a statement that you've been

extorting money from Bronx delicatessens . . . under du-
ress. That the Boston Road Blackies threatened you, that
you were Tyrone Wood's little slave."

"I won't sign. I won't, I won't."

Johnson and McQueen dragged me back to my cage. I
wasn't allowed any visitors. I was an outlaw who didn't have
a single right. "Forget about your mom and dad. They don't
exist." I didn't care what McQueen said. I knew Faigele
would come. But the bulls were much too clever. What if
they hadn't told the dark lady that I was in the caboose? I
began to panic. I'd be stuck forever in some ghostly route
between Simpson Street and Children's Court, the next
stop for a delinquent.

I shut my eyes and prayed that the gods of Boston Road
might deliver me. And when I looked up, Everett Darling
was there, outside the cage. My Samson from the Luxor.

"Baby," he said. "It will be all right."

And then Johnson and McQueen appeared with a third
man. He was dressed like me, in a suit from Feuerman &
Marx. He had silver hair. And I recognized him in an instant.
He was the dentist's younger brother, Stanislaus Staples.

"Ah, we haven't charged him yet, Stanislaus."

"Then I'd call it a miscarriage of justice, Mr. McQueen,
locking up an eleven-year-old boy."

"He's a material witness," Johnson said. "He was at the
scene of the crime . . . holding a precious piece of evidence,
a bat with blood on it."

"Well, are you arresting him or not?"

The two detectives shrugged their shoulders. They were caught in some malicious web that hadn't been of their making. They didn't know what to do. The captain of the precinct arrived, an Irishman who had a puffier face than Johnson and McQueen.

"Hello, Stannie," he said. "How's Meyer?"

And that's when I realized that Stanislaus Staples was the Little Man's lawyer.

"Meyer's in tip-top condition," Stanislaus said. "He isn't a churchgoer, Captain O'Connor. But he's active in temple affairs. And he gets fidgety when a child of the Jewish persuasion is falsely accused and has to sit in a stinking cell."

"It's an accident, Stannie . . . damn you, Johnson, will you get the key?"

Johnson unlocked the cage.

"Come into my office . . . all of you, please."

And we marched into the captain's office: Stanislaus, the two detectives, Samson, and me. I'd seen this captain before. He was a regular at the dentist's poker games.

"Baby," he said, all of a sudden, "how is your darling mother? Johnson, did you notify his mum and dad?"

"We did, Captain. Most certainly."

"Dimwits, I can vouch for the boy. Stannie, did you ever meet his mum? She dealt for Darce, that poor, departed man."

I watched Stanislaus, could see his face tighten. "Captain, we have the living to deal with . . . before we can deal with the dead."

"Didn't mean any harm, Stannie. The little chap was fond of your brother. We all were. He was the most trusted man in the Bronx."

Stanislaus couldn't adore a captain who liked to reminisce. "I presume you haven't done any paperwork on the boy."

"Nothing. Little Charyn was our guest."

"Good. Then there are no records to seal or unseal."

"Stannie, is the kid your client?"

Stanislaus walked past the captain, clutching my arm. "If you should ever invite him to Simpson Street again, I'll sue the pants off the city for abducting a minor."

Samson followed us out of the captain's office. I could hear Johnson mumble. "Makes no sense. We help the Little Man, and we get our fingers slapped."

"Shhh," said Captain O'Connor. "Shut your mouth."

Stanislaus didn't say a word to me.

Faigele met us at the bottom of the stairs. She'd come with Dubbie Yellin, because Dubbie was a high school senior and could understand the language of Simpson Street. Sergeant Sam had stayed home. He was scared to death of police stations, and he must have opted to mind little Marve.

Faigele stared at my homburg and striped suit. She had a madness in her eyes. "Gigolo," she said. "Is that why the police arrested you?"

"He wasn't arrested, Mrs. Charyn."

"Faigele," I said, "this is Stanislaus Staples, Esquire, Darcy's younger brother."

"Skip the esquire, please."

He shook Faigele's hand, introduced himself to Dubbie, and mom came out of her madness in time to notice the resemblance between Stanislaus and Darcy.

"My brother was fond of you, Mrs. Charyn."

"We were at the burial," Faigele said. "I would have remembered seeing you."

"I didn't go, Mrs. Charyn."

"You were away on business?"

"Not at all. My brother was a fool. He martyred himself to the Democratic Party. I could have gotten him out of the Tombs with one phone call. But he was stubborn. He wanted Franklin Delano Roosevelt to redeem him. And I'm afraid the president had decided to forget Darcy Staples . . . I couldn't go to that farce, stand there while the party bosses eulogized a man they'd helped to kill."

"Stanislaus," I said, "he's lying next to Mr. Herman Melville."

"My brother was a big reader, but he shouldn't have buried his nose in books."

Stanislaus touched the brim of his homburg, said goodbye to Faigele, and withdrew from the precinct with Darcy's dancing step. Samson was right behind him.

There were no beatings. Dad didn't even put me in the closet. He was still in a state of shock. Little Marve wheeled his stroller through the apartment. "Jerome's a J.D., Jerome's a J.D."

Dubbie and mom devoured a pack of cigarettes between them. Faigele guzzled dad's schnapps. She had all the wisdom of Belorusse in her blood. She didn't ask me how I'd fallen upon Feuerman & Marx.

"Good," she said. "We won't have to buy you a graduation suit."

I returned to school, expecting more derision about Dumbo, the boy with big ears who'd become a juvenile delinquent. But my classmates looked at me with awe. None of them had been inside the cage at Simpson Street. Diana W. invited me to her Friday night dances. I wouldn't go. I didn't want to take advantage of my sudden status. Rosalind, the beauty of our class, asked the J.D. to walk her home. I did. I wanted to spite Henry Weintraub, her official boyfriend. But I didn't take much pleasure in these little acts of revenge. I couldn't stop thinking of Amanda Little, alias Tyrone Wood.

I went to the cafeteria. Our caid had already changed the decor. There wasn't a single photograph of King Farouk on the cafeteria's walls. The Chesterfield would no longer offend Israel and the Little Man with craven images of an Egyptian king.

The sultan was at his table, sipping celery tonic. He

offered to share with me. But I wouldn't drink from Farouk's bottle.

"You gave up Tyrone to the Little Man, didn't you?"

"Piss-in-the-pants, did I have a choice?"

"Tyrone would have died for you, and you betrayed him. Is it because he's a colored man?"

"It has nothing to do with color. It's Ty's fault. He wouldn't let Meyer's jukeboxes into darktown."

"Boston Road, you mean."

"Meyer threatened to destroy my bottling plants. I wouldn't have a drop of celery tonic. I would have had to close the cafeteria."

"Sultan," I said. "You survived Corregidor. You could have survived a soda drought."

I left the sultan with his bottle, took the crosstown bus, and stood outside the Luxor, stalking Everett Darling. I didn't want to confront him in the cave. He would only have lied with Luke and Mur around him. One with the little hole in his heart and the other with the wigs of Hedy Lamarr.

I craved the dark, but I didn't sneak inside to catch ten minutes of Garfield as the lawyer who betrays his brother in *Force of Evil*. I suffered with Garfield from film to film. He was like the mirror of what adulthood would mean. Money and love. Money and love.

Samson crept out of the dark on my third trip to the Luxor. He wasn't that rough giant who'd forsaken the larger world. He was wearing a camel's-hair coat. I followed him to the Lewis Morris, the *only* building on the Concourse that had the dimensions of a Park Avenue palace. The doorman saluted him. I waited half a minute.

"Delivery," I muttered, "for Mr. Darling."

"Ah," the doorman said. "You're lucky to catch him. Suite Nineteen J."

I didn't even smile when I discovered "Luxor Enterprises" painted on Samson's door.

I went in without knocking. Samson sat behind a mahogany desk.

"What took you so long? I could spot you half a mile away."

"I'm a kid," I said. "I stand out. And you're Meyer Lansky's middle man. The Luxor is a front."

"No. I love that theater."

"But you don't really live in the dark. You're a Bronx millionaire, aren't you? And you probably have an interest in Farouk's bottling company."

"It's complicated. I invest."

"For Farouk and the Little Man."

"Mozart composed symphonies when he was six . . . I memorized the music of the market. I won't dare invest for Meyer. A man might get mangled. We do it like a game . . . with Monopoly money."

"You called Stanislaus, didn't you?"

"I had to correct Meyer's mistake. His men thought you

were one of Tyrone's brats, a mulatto with light skin. But Meyer wouldn't let a Jewish boy rot in jail."

"Where's Tyrone?"

"Baby," he said, "how can I call Meyer and ask him that?"

"But I can."

Of course I couldn't. I got the name and number of Stanislaus' firm from Ev. I called him. "Baby Charyn," I shouted to his secretary.

Stanislaus picked up the phone.

"Counselor, can we meet?"

Stanislaus' limousine waited outside P.S. 61 the next afternoon. I didn't act like a diva in front of Henry Weintraub and Rosalind. I crept into the car and we rode down to Wall Street, watching the sun begin to slink over the Hudson like a burning ball while I sat on the smoothest cushions and had an Eskimo Pie from the limo's fridge.

Stanislaus had an office on Liberty Street. The typists and accountants and clerks marveled that Meyer Lansky's lawyer would make an appointment with a kid from public school.

But my appearance didn't please him. It seemed to rekindle the haunted life of his brother.

"Charyn, I won't give any secrets away. And I'm not talking lawyer-client privilege. Mr. Lansky has many lawyers."

"But I have to know what happened to Tyrone Wood. He was my friend."

Stanislaus picked up a silver paper knife, scratched behind his ear. "You visited Darcy in the Tombs, didn't you?"

"Yes. Me and Faigele did."

"What was his cell like?"

"It had an armchair and electric coffeepot. The food stank. Mom baked him a Russian coffee cake."

"And what was Darcy's comment . . . about the cake?"

"It was a long time ago, Counselor."

"What did he say?"

" 'It's a dream.' "

"That's Darce . . . you and your mother were the last to see him alive. Should I tell you how many beatings he saved me from? How many . . ."

Stanislaus put down the paper knife, dialed a number, talked into the phone, then stared into my eyes. "Your black chief is dead. He's lying in some unmarked grave. And don't ask me to clarify the Little Man's affairs. I can't."

"He got into the gangsters' car because of me."

"Charyn, I wasn't there."

"He knew Meyer's men would have shot my head off if he put up a struggle."

"Probably. He was brave and brash, like my brother . . . come on, Charyn. Let's eat. We'll cry on each other's shoulder."

Stanislaus grabbed his homburg, and we rushed out of his office at five o'clock, long before dinnertime. His driver brought us up to the theater district, and Stanislaus knocked on the window of a restaurant on Forty-sixth

Street. It was called Barbetta's. There didn't seem to be much life inside Barbetta's doors.

"Mario," Stanislaus said, with repeated raps on the window, "it's me."

Finally a man appeared at the window, smiled, and motioned us into the restaurant. First he had to unlock the doors.

"Ah," the man said, "Mr. Stanislaus, what a pleasure."

"I'm incorrigible," Stanislaus said. "But I can't resist. I love to 'open' your restaurant. And meet my protégé. Little Charyn."

"Is he clerking for you, Mr. Stanislaus?"

"Perhaps. One day."

"Then I'd better watch my language around two lawyers."

It was like a Garden of Eden inside Barbetta's. It had a fountain and huge, hanging plants, and we had the whole restaurant to ourselves. We sat at a round table with candlesticks and a white cloth that was like an embroidered masterpiece. Stanislaus didn't even have to order. Mario arrived with a decanter of wine. Stanislaus tasted the wine, and when he saw my own sad hunger, that urge to skip junior high and James Monroe and become an adult, like Garfield on and off the screen, like Darcy, dead or alive, Stanislaus said, "What the hell. Mario, pour my protégé a drink."

Mario obliged us. "But we'll have to be careful, Mr. Stanislaus, when the other customers arrive. Or I'll lose my liquor license."

"I'll get you ten liquor licenses for every one you lose. Mario, who sits behind the mayor's throne, runs City Hall?"

"Mr. Lansky."

Stanislaus touched Mario's collar. "Call him the Little Man. It's much more discreet."

"Right, Mr. Stanislaus. It won't happen again."

I sipped the wine. It wasn't celery tonic. But how could a restaurant on Forty-sixth Street have been part of Farouk's franchise? Soda made with celery roots. That was a Bronx affair.

Stanislaus finished the first decanter of wine. A second one appeared. We ate a salad. I watched him cut the lettuce leaves with all the art of a surgeon. I couldn't copy him. Stanislaus laughed when I tried to saw a lettuce leaf with my knife.

"Charyn," he said, "we're *en famille* here. Use your fingers."

"But it wouldn't be polite. And what's 'en famille'?"

"A meal where you don't have to worry who's looking over your shoulder."

I clinked glasses with him. "En famille!"

And suddenly, this man who could boss a police station started to shake. "I miss my brother . . . we're both mourners, aren't we, Charyn? Did Boston Road ask you to pick a street name? . . . well, give forth."

"Stanislaus, I'd feel disloyal to Tyrone. You work for the man who killed him."

"But that's privileged information. And I had nothing against Tyrone. Give!"

"Delilah," I said.

"That's grand. Guard it with your life."

We had noodles with vegetables and a creamy red sauce that was nothing like mom's Russian macaroni. We had grilled fish, a fruit salad, and cups of bittersweet black coffee with little macaroons.

Mario didn't present us with a bill. We got up from the table as other customers began to arrive.

"Charyn," Stanislaus said. "I'm soused. Will you bring me my man?"

I wobbled out of the restaurant and returned with Stanislaus' driver, who bundled him up and helped him into the car while Mario's customers stared at us. Could they have understood our grief? That we really were in mourning. And for a moment, Stanislaus needed to be around a schoolboy who'd once been part of his brother's life. I was the last trace of Darcy that Stanislaus had. And I didn't need Garfield or the comfort of a silver screen. I'd drunk wine with Stanislaus from the same decanter, and I was at least a little bit of a man.

THE BLACK SWAN

Family portrait at the Black Swan: Harvey, Dad (holding little Marve), Faigele, and Jerome.

Dad was in and out of difficulty. He could craft a fur coat but he wasn't a tycoon, like Everett Darling . . . or King Farouk. He became an entrepreneur, and our finances fell into quicksand. Faigele had to go back to work. But how much could she make at her old job as cherry dipper in a chocolate factory? The summer was coming and we had another mouth to feed, little Marve; she couldn't subject him to a Bronx heat wave, which was more brutal than the Sahara.

Mom could only use whatever skills she had. She was a fabled card dealer, thanks to Darcy, even though she hadn't dealt in years. She wouldn't advertise herself. But one day, out of the blue, mom received a letter from the Black Swan, the most celebrated casino and country club in the Catskill Mountains. It was at the Black Swan where Jerry Lewis first performed and where Eddie Fisher, the Philadelphia heartthrob, had his big chance. Located in a little upstate "archipelago," between Monticello and Liberty, New York, it was part of the Borscht Belt, that vacation ground for Jews from Brooklyn and the Bronx; with all its bungalow colonies, casinos, and country clubs, it must have had the densest population in the world during July and August. And Faigele had just been hired by the Black Swan to deal at its big casino. Gambling wasn't strictly legal in 1949, and mom had to wear the title of "hostess." Her contract was the talk of our entire neighborhood. As a married woman she didn't have to live in the employees' dorm. The Black Swan lent her quarters at the bungalow colony it maintained. Our bungalow was on a hill overlooking the country club itself. It had a name, the Hawk's Nest, and was the equivalent of a tiny mansion. Faigele invited Dubbie to spend the summer with us. Dubbie abandoned all her boyfriends to become a seventeen-year-old belle at the Black Swan.

I had my own room, of course, and free access to all the Black Swan's recreational facilities. But I was boiling. I wanted to stay in the Bronx and plot my revenge. I'd sit at Addie Vallin's until the Little Man arrived, christen him with an ice-cream soda, toss a black and tan in his face, and shout in full majesty, "Meyer, Tyrone Wood is kissing you from the dark side of the grave."

I didn't care what the Little Man did to me, as long as he realized that he couldn't kill the caid of Boston Road just like that. But Faigele said I had to go to the mountains with her. "Think of Marve, think of Marve," dad said as he chased me around the apartment. "He could catch polio in this lousy, stinking sun." And so I went to the Catskills with all the bitterness of an unrequited boy.

We were lords of the bungalow colony. We didn't have to shop at Monticello. Twice a week a grocery clerk would deliver food from the Black Swan's freezer, and mom also had meal tickets for the soda fountain and main dining room. Dad, who had nothing to do, was given the soft drink concession near the Black Swan's tennis courts. A truck arrived from New York City, bearing fifty cases of Farouk's celery soda. I reasoned with myself. The Black Swan was an outpost of the Bronx. Why should it be deprived of the Bronx's favorite drink? I was glad about the celery tonic until I noticed the driver of the truck. It was Dan O'Brien of Engine 42, with all his good-natured blondness.

"Dan," I said, "it's me, Baby Charyn. Why aren't you out chasing fires?"

"Ah," he said, "I like to moonlight during the summer season."

"Did the sultan hire you? King Farouk?"

"Don't know any Farouks. It was the man I rescued from that movie house. Mr. Darling."

I didn't feel like investigating Dan. He'd been kind to Baby, had welcomed him inside Engine 42 when Baby was freezing his pants off.

"Have a soda with me," I said. We went into the casino, sat at the fountain. My face started to freeze when I saw the soda jerk. The caid of Boston Road had come back from the dead. He was wearing a bowtie and the little pointed cap of his new profession. And with him was Paula, his best little fox, who had her own pointed cap. I wanted to hug Tyrone . . . and strangle him for not telling me that he was still alive. But I couldn't show my feelings in front of Fireman Dan. Tyrone wouldn't be here with his fox unless he had a powerful reason. And I wouldn't give his secrets away.

"Two black and tans," I said.

Tyrone didn't even blink. He and Paula prepared the ice-cream sodas. But I couldn't control my venom.

"Dan," I said, "meet Cool Papa Bell . . . the king of colored baseball. He used to play for the Kansas City Monarchs until they sold him to the Black Swan."

The fireman shook Tyrone's hand. "Glad to meet you. But Baby, I don't get it. How can a team sell a player to a resort hotel?"

"It's easy," I said. "The Monarchs banished him for violating his contract. Papa wouldn't play ball. So the Monarchs put him on the market. There was only one bidder. The Black Swan."

"Papa," Dan said, "is that the truth?"

"It's close enough. Would you like another black and tan?"

Dan wanted to pay, but I wouldn't let him.

"Fireman, it's on the house."

I left Tyrone ten cents as a tip and walked Dan back to his truck. "That Cool Papa Bell makes a mean ice-cream soda."

"Will you visit us again?"

"I can't promise," he said. "Mr. Darling never gives me my routes in advance."

I didn't want Dan to leave. But Ev was paying him by the hour. And Dan had more deliveries to make.

"Good-bye, Jerome."

And when the truck disappeared down the street, I started to cry. I couldn't seem to get accustomed to mourning a live man. I fiddled around, sharpened the tooth of my top, and went behind the big casino, where the earth was hard as concrete and could accommodate the "bite" of a digger. But I didn't even get to wind the string. Tyrone swiped the digger out of my hand. I wasn't scared.

"Been waiting for you, Ty."

He took the dime I'd left him and pressed it into my cheek. It hurt like hell.

"Little man, did I ever show you disrespect?"

"Meyer Lansky's the Little Man, not me . . . and couldn't you have made one phone call, even if you were supposed to be under the ground? I was worried to death."

"That's no excuse. You shouldn't have tipped me in front of a total stranger . . . here's what I think of your money."

He wound up like Satchel Paige, tossed the dime into the air, and while I watched it hop over the casino roof like a tiny silver dish, Tyrone punched me in the mouth.

"Don't you ever, ever mock the name of Cool Papa Bell."

But the punch only brought out more of my venom. "Sorry," I said. "Should I have called you Josh Gibson, the soda jerk?"

Tyrone punched me again. "There's nothing dishonorable about jerking fizzy water at a soda fountain. And should I tell you what happened to Josh? He died in an insane asylum . . . after hitting a thousand home runs. He kept having conversations in his head with Joe DiMaggio. 'Why don't you talk to me, Joe?' And him, the greatest player who ever lived . . . how could I telephone? I've been racing a typhoon since I lost you outside that delicatessen."

I couldn't stop blubbering.

"Crybaby," he said. "I didn't hit you that hard."

"It's not the hurt. I'm just glad you're alive."

He touched the dent in my cheek that the dime had made. "Ah, Delilah, my best little man."

And pretty soon we were both crying like crazy people.

"It's Farouk's fault," I said. "He sold you down the river."

"You can't blame him. The Chesterfield's one little oasis in Meyer's territory."

"But Boston Road belongs to you."

"Not now."

"Didn't you escape Meyer's men?"

"Only because they got greedy. They rode that hearse of theirs right to Meyer's usual dumping ground. They had their shovels. But they couldn't resist. 'Colored boy,' they said, 'why don't you empty your pockets?' And I did. I took out my wallet gun. It's the oldest trick in the world."

"What's a wallet gun?"

Tyrone reached into his pants and pulled out a wallet. Only it wasn't a wallet. It was a gun encased in deerskin, with a hole in the middle for the trigger.

"I shot Meyer's number-one goon in the heart and I sold the others back to the Little Man."

"But why didn't they search your pockets after you were dead?"

"Because it wouldn't have given them any pleasure. They had to rob me first. And Meyer was mad as hell. But he had to ransom his own goons or he couldn't have shown his face at Addie Vallin's."

"Then you won," I said.

"No. It's like nigger baseball. Josh could have socked ten thousand home runs, and he'd still be talking to Joe DiMaggio in his head . . . you can't pull a coup on the Little Man and not pay the price. He would have declared war on the Blackies and scalped all my foxes. Once I took the ransom money, I had to sell him Boston Road . . . and disappear. I'm Meyer's most wanted little man."

"But Tyrone, you picked the wrong country club. The Black Swan is king of the Catskills. Meyer has to know where you are."

"I want him to know. It's called hiding in plain sight. If I really vanished, he'd scorch the earth looking for me. Now he can relax and pretend I don't exist."

"Does he own the Black Swan?"

"It wouldn't startle me."

"Did he hire my mom?"

"I doubt it. Meyer has his fingers in too many pies. He couldn't manage the Black Swan."

"Then who hired her?"

"It's a mystery."

"Couldn't we clear it up, Ty? . . . and give me back my digger, please?"

"I'd like to borrow it for a while . . . have to sleep with one eye open at the Swan. If a man gets too nosy I can scrape him with that digger of yours."

"Keep it," I said. "But tell me the truth. Did you really abandon Boston Road?"

He smiled. "What's a Blackie without his neighborhood? I ordered my lieutenants to cooperate with Meyer . . . and give him nothing. I adopted my own scorched-earth policy. Meyer gets his jukeboxes, but not even the loneliest nigger will listen to the Little Man's music. And money means everything to Meyer. If he starts losing dollars, he'll get disgusted and pull out his boxes."

"I knew it," I said. "You're still the caid of Boston Road."

"Calm down. And do me a favor. Don't visit the Swan's soda shop. Because if you sit at the counter and start ordering black and tans, Meyer's goons will have to start noticing me."

"But will I ever see you again?"

"In the shadows," Tyrone said. "Not at the Swan's main canteen."

And he took off with my digger in his hand. I stood there, lonely as hell. Because not even a fortune of Feuerman suits could replace a friend.

I didn't betray Tyrone. I avoided the soda fountain. But I'd sit with mom at the other end of the casino, watch her deal with a cigarette in her mouth, Dubbie beside her, clutching little Marve. They'd natter and laugh like a couple of card sharks. I'd never seen Mom so happy. She'd walk arm in arm with Dubbie when she wasn't dealing.

Mom drove the other dealers out of business. Players would book her a week in advance. They didn't even have to mention Faigele. "I want the Black Swan."

I began to recognize old familiar faces. Mom could have been dealing for Darcy again. Fred R. Lions arrived and reserved his seat at mom's table. Judges I remembered from 1944 showed up. Millionaires would neglect their wives, their mistresses, and their suites at other Catskill resorts to play poker with the Black Swan. Gangsters appeared, but not the Little Man himself. "Meyer's superstitious," the gangsters said. He brought his own dealer whenever he played. But the Little Man had his "proxy." Stanislaus Staples.

Stanislaus began to visit mom's table during our second

week at the Swan. It troubled mom, because it was like dealing to Darcy's ghost. But soon Stanislaus imposed his own personality upon the game. He didn't pretend to be his brother. He wasn't a party chief. Stanislaus wouldn't curry to the Democrats. He was Lansky's lawyer. And if a gangster whistled at mom or asked Dubbie for a date, Stanislaus would drop a poker chip in that gangster's lap.

"Save the romance, friend. You're insulting Mrs. Charyn and her niece."

"Stannie, who appointed you sheriff of this game?"

"The Little Man."

And all the rancor and rowdiness would come to a halt. Mom got used to Stanislaus, was grateful he was around. But I was smoldering. Stanislaus gathered his chips and left the game for a moment to share a celery tonic with me.

"What's wrong?"

"Stanislaus, you wined and dined me and it was all a big act. You took advantage of a kid."

"Enlighten me," he said, with the dentist's lilt in his voice.

"Didn't you swear that Tyrone Wood was in an unmarked grave?"

"Indeed I did."

"Then have a look at the soda fountain. What do you see?"

"Exactly what I said. A man who's in an unmarked grave."

"Is that what you'd call a soda jerk at the Black Swan?"

"I would. Because that soda jerk is trapped in a grave that's a little roomier than most. But it's a matter of words. Baby, I promise you, he has nowhere to go."

And Stanislaus returned to the game.

I was humbled. Because Stanislaus could pull the truth out of a handkerchief. Lawyers like him didn't know how to lie.

The game heated up. And Faigele had to deal six afternoons and seven nights a week. Her salary was a pittance compared to what the players gave her personally for the right to sit at her table. It was like a lucky lightning bolt. We were growing rich without IBM. Faigele was her own commodity. The players were delirious when she sang out the cards without upsetting the cigarette in her mouth.

"Mr. Lions, I believe you have a possible flush."

"Fannie dear, we shouldn't have ostracized you. Would you like to return to the Democrats? Boss Flynn would take you back into the fold."

"Concentrate on your cards, Mr. Lions."

Our borough president loved to suffer around the dark lady. And then another sufferer arrived. King Farouk. He began quoting Shakespeare the second he had his chips. "Milady, I'll die, I'll die, if I don't have you for a little hour."

"King," Stanislaus said, "behave, or I'll throw you to the killer swans."

Farouk bulged in his chair. "What killer swans?"

"The United Jewish Appeal. They'd love to devour King Farouk . . . they have their own table at the casino."

But Farouk wouldn't let go of that hump on his back, King Richard's hump.

"Stannie," he said, "isn't that my man at the soda fountain, my vassal, who murders for me from time to time?"

"Farouk, you're blind."

"But I'd swear it's my own colored charmer."

"I said you're blind."

Faigele couldn't understand all the banter at the card table. She looked at me, and I rolled my eyes. It was a signal we had in 1944, when there was potential damage to Darcy or his game.

"Mr. Farouk," mom said, "one more peep, and you'll have to cash in your chips."

Farouk didn't even appeal to Dubbie, the only one at the table who could talk Shakespeare with him. Dubbie was on Faigele's side. And he couldn't bear the terror of being banished from the Catskills' most significant game.

It was like a madhouse. People would line up at the soda fountain, begging for black and tans, and I felt sorry for Farouk's ex-bodyguard, the most visible invisible man I ever saw. I kept away, like I'd promised Tyrone. But the sultan couldn't survive without an ice-cream soda. His fanny was so broad, it took up two seats at the fountain. Stanislaus had sworn him to silence, and he didn't dare address Tyrone by name. "Kid," he'd growl. "Mr. Soda Jerk. I'll have a double black and tan."

I could hear him across the casino. And for a moment I wished the sultan had died in Corregidor. But I wasn't Farouk's favorite humpbacked king, who lived only for spite. And if Farouk had perished, I wouldn't have met Tyrone. Still, I couldn't bear watching gangsters and politicians and fat millionaires run Ty off his feet. I had to get away from the Black Swan.

Faigele's new wealth had spilled off on me. I had twenty dollars in my pants, the spoils of one afternoon at mom's poker game. I got on the bus to Monticello. I was like a drug addict, desperate to watch a movie. Monticello had a pair of movie houses, and I planned to kill the day and catch whatever was playing.

You couldn't enter Monticello without noticing a giant billboard of the White Rock Girl. She was daring in 1949, because the White Rock Girl wore a diaphanous gown and anyone could peek at her breasts. She had wings on her shoulders and stood on a white rock, with a bubbling silver spring below her that was supposed to represent the purity of White Rock club soda, the biggest seller in all of Sullivan County, *after* Farouk's tonic. Farouk didn't have to advertise with angels on a billboard. "My soda," he liked to say, "speaks for itself."

I passed the marquees of the Broadway and the Rialto, and I was a bit surprised, because John Garfield had come to Monticello like a summer storm and captured both movie houses. *Force of Evil* was at the Rialto, and *Body and Soul* was at the Broadway. I bought a pack of Life

Savers and abandoned the White Rock Girl to watch Joe Morse, the mob lawyer in *Force of Evil*, prepare to grab the numbers racket and make it legal. But his big brother, Leo, is one of the numbers bankers that Joe has to ruin before he can take over the rackets. He tries to warn Leo. "I'll make you rich with an office on Wall Street up in the clouds." Leo won't listen. He dies in the middle of a mob war. And Joe himself is ruined. "I'm dead, disbarred," he tells Leo's former secretary, who reminded me of the White Rock Girl without wings.

"When did it happen?" she asks.

"The day I was born."

I knew I wanted to be a mob lawyer, like Joe Morse . . . and Stanislaus Staples. Both of them had offices on Wall Street and had Phi Beta Kappa keys suspended from a chain on their vests (I was too young to understand what that key meant). Both of them wore "signature" suits from Feuerman & Marx. Stanislaus' features were much finer than Joe's. And he was a Protestant in a Catholic and Jewish culture. But they had the same disturbingly sad eyes.

It was almost dark when I returned to the Black Swan. The program at the Broadway and the Rialto began to trouble me. There seemed to be a familiar hand behind that double bill of John Garfield, a hand that had reached from the Bronx.

Mom hadn't missed Baby. She was dealing at the casino. I went to Rusty, the manager, a guy in his fifties who sported a red toupee. I was the cat's meow to him, the kid who belonged to Faigele's menagerie.

"Rusty," I asked, "when did the Black Swan open?"

"During the war," he said. " 'Forty-two, I think."

I didn't need a lightning bolt. It was clear as celery soda . . . or the White Rock Girl's diaphanous gown. The Black Swan wasn't named after some idol of the Borscht Belt. It was a fantasm fresh out of Hollywood, during the darkest year of the war. The Black Swan was a pirate ship that billowed in the huge water tanks at 20th Century Fox. The very idea of it must have excited my three cellar rats. Everett, Luke, and Mur adored swashbucklers and were mad about Tyrone Power, Fox's biggest star, who plays a pirate in *The Black Swan*, the box-office bonanza of 1942. Only Ev would have been diabolic enough to dub a Catskill casino "the Black Swan."

I searched the grounds. They weren't within a mile of the Swan. Perhaps the cellar rats were hiding in plain sight, like Tyrone Wood. I went back to Monticello, but I couldn't find them in the bowels of the Broadway or the Rialto.

I knew they were near. All I had to do was wait. But something intervened. The Black Swan lost its fabulous soda jerk. Tyrone vanished from the fountain. And it was dangerous for him. The Little Man couldn't brag that he could kill Tyrone whenever he wanted, that the caid of Boston Road only breathed because of him.

It was Stanislaus who told me what had happened. Two drunken dishwashers wandered into Ty's black dormitory at the Swan, wanted to fondle Paula and rob Tyrone of his tips. The caid had slashed them with a knife, and the dishwashers were lying in a Monticello hospital. It would have been one more summer crime. But the dishwashers weren't black. They were locals, backwoods people who lived on a dirt road behind the casino. And the sheriff of Sullivan County couldn't idle. He had to bag "that soda shop nigger" or lose the next election. His deputies swarmed through the Black Swan.

Rusty covered all the card tables with a big cloth. He didn't want the deputies to close him down. But the sheriff arrived in his polished boots, an enormous Smith & Wesson strapped to his pants. His name was Billy Trumps.

"Where's that Faigele, Mrs. Fannie?" he snarled.

"In Catskill heaven," Stanislaus said. He wasn't frightened of a country sheriff.

"Then I'll have to knock on heaven's door," said Billy Trumps. He was staring at King Farouk. "Ain't you Fatso Levine, who won the Medal of Honor and marched with Skinny Wainwright across Corregidor?"

"I'm King Farouk."

"I was with the Marines," said Billy Trumps. "And only a fool and a coward would disremember that march . . . I have half a mind to arrest the entire table."

"On what charge?" asked Stanislaus.

"Insulting Skinny and the Pacific war . . . and gambling on the premises."

"Do you know who I am?" asked Fred R. Lions, his fingers shaking. "Bronx borough president and a Democratic Party chief."

"Then it will be a pleasure, sir, leading you to jail."

Stanislaus stirred in his seat, but the dark lady touched his hand and smiled at the sheriff. "I'm Mrs. Fannie," she said.

"Why didn't you say so? Would you allow this humble lawman into your game?"

Faigele threw off Rusty's cloth and exposed the card table.

"Can I have some chips, ma'am?"

"As many as you like," Faigele said.

"But first he has to 'fess up that he's Fatso Levine."

"I'm King Farouk."

Stanislaus glared at the sultan, who began to shrink inside his blubber. "I was once Lieutenant Levine . . . of Corregidor."

And the sultan instantly lost his status and his mysterious mien. It didn't matter that he was a millionaire soda baron, that he had his own cafeteria, and an enterprise that had pushed the White Rock Girl into second place. Billy Trumps had unmasked him. He wasn't Farouk anymore. He was Fatso Levine with a medal that he'd tucked away somewhere.

"Fatso," said Fred R. Lions, "you're holding the high card . . . you in or out?"

But Faigele had seen the distress in Fatso's slumping body. "Mr. Lions," she said, "are you the dealer?"

"No, Fannie darling."

"Then don't give lessons to the players . . . King Farouk, are you betting, or will you stand pat with your queen high?"

"Forgive me, Faigele," he said, and got up from the table. Shakespeare couldn't help him now. He had his bottling plants, but not even Richard the Third's missing horse could have rescued the kingdom of his own name.

Billy Trumps held his bottom card tight to his chest, smiled at mom, and started to brag. "You know what kinda knife that nigger had? It was sharp as the devil, and two feet long, like a Jap sword. He'll get ten years when we catch him. Monticello magistrates aren't fond of colored riffraff that come into our county and do bodily harm . . . but I didn't mean to pontificate, Mrs. Fannie, and ruin the tempo of the game. Would you make a lonesome lawman happy and have dinner with him tonight?"

Stanislaus had to stand up and whisper in Billy Trump's ear.

The sheriff blinked and tossed in his cards. "Duty calls," he said. "Pleased to meet you, Mrs. Fannie."

He collected his earnings at Rusty's little bank and marched out of the casino. Faigele called a twenty-minute recess. Stanislaus stood by himself and smoked a Fatima. I went up to him.

"Stanislaus, what did you say that turned Billy Trumps into a ghost?"

"Nothing much. I told him that Faigele was Meyer's fiancée."

"That's ridiculous. Mom's already married."

"Ah," Stanislaus said. "It's tough-guy talk . . . fiancée means a mistress in gangland, a regular girl."

"But mom doesn't even know the Little Man. And you could destroy her reputation."

"But isn't it better than having Billy Trumps wait outside your mother's window every midnight like a moonstruck animal?"

"I suppose. But you still shouldn't have said that about her. Mom isn't Meyer's mistress."

Stanislaus returned to his law practice in Manhattan and came back to the Swan next weekend with his wife, Helen, and his son, Leicester, who was around my age and went to boarding school in Vermont. He must have been guilty about the damage he might have done to Faigele, because he had a present for little Charyn. A Daisy "Red Ryder" beebee gun that had the same lever-action loader as Red Ryder, the comic book cowboy. I was the envy of every brat at the Black Swan, except Leicester himself, who didn't have a high regard for beebee guns.

"It's for infants and brutes," Leicester said. He was tall

and lanky and ran around in white bucks and tennis shorts. Stanislaus hoped that Leicester might become my friend. But Leicester snubbed me and the Swan. He and his mother were terrific snobs. A Catskill resort for them was as unremarkable as a zoo. Helen Staples had short blond hair and must have belonged to some aristocracy I'd never heard about. She took off with Leicester in Stanislaus' limousine to play golf at a posh club, where Jewish gangsters weren't welcome. She wouldn't even shake hands with the dark lady, who was a common gambler in her eyes.

Stanislaus was miserable. "Shouldn't have brought them," he said. "It's not their particular paradise. I'm sorry."

"It's nothing, Stanislaus. And I'm the winner. I have a beautiful gun."

I went hunting in the fields behind the Black Swan. I wasn't Red Ryder, but I mastered that lever action and banged away until I knocked a chipmunk out of the trees. I beat the grass with my Daisy, looking for the chipmunk's corpse, and while I was slapping here and there, somebody picked me up and hurled me over a little rock wall.

It was Tyrone Wood.

"Ty," I said. "I'm so glad to see you."

"I'm not. Shame on you and your kind. Shooting little animals like some great white bwana."

"What's a 'bwana,' Ty?"

"A foolish white man who thinks the whole world's his private jungle."

"Did you really use a Jap sword on the two drunken dishwashers?"

"Jap sword? I had your digger. And those dishwashers weren't that drunk. I think it was a courtesy call. The Little Man was sending me his regards."

"But they weren't from Manhattan. That's what the sheriff said."

"The Little Man doesn't need Manhattan. He can borrow local talent. That sheriff is in Meyer's pocket."

"Where's Paula?"

"I couldn't leave her here. I had a Blackie drop her in Pennsylvania with one of my aunts."

"Why didn't you go with her?"

"And get us all killed?"

"But I thought the Little Man would leave you alone while you were hiding in plain sight."

"I thought so too. But he must have been jealous."

"Jealous of what?"

"My black and tans. How could he humiliate a soda jerk whose reputation was beginning to grow? Customers were leaving Addie Vallin's, I swear, and trekking up to Monticello to taste one of my black and tans. It must have irked the Little Man. He couldn't sit at my counter. He would have had to beg me with his eyes for a black and tan. He had the goddamn sheriff send the dishwashers to break my thumbs so I couldn't jerk ice-cream sodas at the Swan."

"Ty," I said, "that Mr. Lansky is a conniving, complicated man. Run the hell away from here."

"How? He'll never figure that I haven't disappeared from the Swan. But I'm starving, little man. I haven't eaten in six days, except for huckleberries . . . and apples I picked from the trees."

And so I sneaked him food from the Black Swan's kitchen and our own icebox. We'd meet in an old, abandoned barn that must have housed horses and cows before the Black Swan was born in 1942.

"Ty," I said, "what happens when the summer's over and I have to go back to school?"

"Little man, a Boston Road Blackie always does a day at a time . . . but you can't spend your afternoons with me. The sheriff might get suspicious."

"But I have my Red Ryder. He'll think I'm hunting chipmunks."

"And his own hunters will come and hunt for me."

"But what's the Black Swan without you, Ty? One big poker game."

"Then you'll have to attach yourself to poker . . . and hide in plain sight."

I was bored, but it wasn't that bad. I liked stealing food. I followed Ty's instructions and hovered like a hawk over mom's card table. And it was Stanislaus who had to suffer. He brought some bitter melancholy down upon himself when his son and wife decided to visit the game. Leicester and handsome Helen, who must have been drinking mint juleps at her golf club. Her eyes couldn't seem to move in the same direction. Leicester had to hold her arm, or she might have crashed to the casino floor.

"Stannie," she said, "can't I play?"

"No, Helen."

She wiggled a finger at mom. "Then how else can I meet the famous Fannie Charyn?"

"Leicester," Stanislaus said, "do your dad a favor and bring Helen up to the big house." The big house was a bone-white mansion where the Swan's ritziest guests stayed in suites with marble bathtubs and balconies that wrapped around a whole corner, and had heartbreaking views of Monticello's American Alps. But Leicester clung to Helen and smirked, ballasting her with his own body. I hated him more than I hated Meyer, who wasn't a snob and had enough sense to be a connoisseur of black and tans.

"Stannie," Helen said, "be kind and let me sit at your whore's table."

The blood drained out of Stanislaus. He stood up and smacked Helen across the face. Leicester couldn't hold her. She dropped like a stone and started to snore.

Stanislaus sat down again. "Faigele," he said, "please forgive my family . . . and deal."

Mom called out the cards, but how could she concentrate with Stanislaus' wife snoring at her feet?

"Queen of spades," she muttered.

"Faigele," said Fred R. Lions, "that's a king."

Stanislaus left his chips on the table, stooped, gathered

Helen in his arms, and carried her up to the big house, with Leicester trailing in his tennis shorts, the mountains looming above them in their own glorious green mist. The Catskills couldn't have cared less about the foibles of one human being. But mom was shivering, and so was I. We were both in love with a mob lawyer, who was more gallant than anyone alive, even if he'd slapped his wife. We could read his calvary, the pain he'd have to endure. His halting walk with Helen was like the stations of an impossible cross. We were almost grateful when Stanislaus stepped onto the porch and was swallowed up by the big house. It meant that we no longer had to look. But mom and I hadn't lost our secret language. We were all alone with a slap that continued to rebound across the lightning crispness of country air.

MONTICELLO ENDING

Muscleman and cha-cha dancer Harvey Charyn,
just before his sojourn in Monticello.

We might have been an ignorant little nation from the dunes of the East Bronx, but we had enough worldliness to know that there was *another* Monticello, the mansion that Thomas Jefferson had built on a little mountain in Virginia. The Black Swan's big house was modeled after his Monticello. Jefferson was a philosopher, like Socrates and Voltaire, and a democrat who might have imagined a twentieth century where mongrels and outlaws could educate themselves and build a new Monticello in the Catskills, with a mountain hotel called the Black Swan.

I didn't have much to do with the big house. I wasn't a paying guest. I didn't wear white bucks, and mom wasn't an aristocrat like Helen Staples. We had our bungalow, the Hawk's Nest, and it didn't have white pillars, balconies, bull's-eye windows, and an octagonal dome that could have belonged to a lighthouse on a hill. But the dome was always dark, as if it were like a dungeon in the sky. That dome was none of my business . . . until I saw bits of light in its own bull's-eye window. And like some dream walker, I drifted down the bungalow colony hill and up that little winding mountain to the big house of the Black Swan.

The busboys saluted me. I could have been young Tom Jefferson, one more Catskill democrat. I climbed right up to the attic, entered the octagonal room. I wasn't surprised. My three cellar rats were sitting in leather chairs, puffing on Fatimas, like kings of the mountain.

"Baby," Samson said. "We're not criminals. This is our vacation . . . a week in the Catskills."

"Sure. The three of you just happened to inherit Monticello's tower."

"We don't have to answer to a little snot nose," Luke said.

Delilah nudged the giant. "I never liked him, Ev."

"And I suppose you didn't flood Monticello with John Garfield flicks."

"That's not illegal," the giant said.

"Or steal from Thomas Jefferson when you had this house built."

"Ev," Luke muttered, "he's giving me a migraine."

"And name the whole shebang after a pirate ship . . . the Black Swan."

Delilah frowned at me. "Ev, he's got an evil mind."

"Does Meyer own this plantation?"

"Baby," Samson said, "it's not clear who has title to the

Black Swan. It's sort of a mishmash . . . Democrats, King Farouk, ourselves, the Little Man. I was only the agent."

"And did you hire my mom to deal?"

"Don't be foolish. Why would we want you at the Swan? To poke into our past? It was Stannie's idea."

"Stanislaus?" I said.

"He took pity on you and your mother, heard about her plight. I recommended a different dealer. But Stannie said no. We argued. He prevailed."

"Then mom and I are his summer babies."

"Something like that," Samson said.

And I left them in the tower. I was sick of them and the Swan. I returned to the Hawk's Nest. But I didn't have much peace. A bronze god drifted into the bungalow. I blinked at him.

"Baby, what the hell are you looking at?"

It was Harve, who'd come all the way from Arizona. But it wasn't the Harve I remembered, an asthmatic boy who loved to fight, but was still an invalid. He'd grown muscles in the land of Aztec sun. He was fourteen years old, and his breathing was as solid as mine.

"What did you do to dad?"

"Nothing," I said.

"You and mom have banished him to the edge of the earth."

"Harvey, he has the soft drink stand near the tennis courts."

"He sells green piss."

"That's not piss, Harve. It's celery soda."

"And why aren't you helping him?"

"It's my vacation. I have to recover from school."

"What about dad's vacation? Couldn't you spell him for a couple of hours, let him swim or read a book."

"Dad hasn't read a book in his life."

"Because he's been busy feeding you."

"That's not fair."

"Fair? You learnt the alphabet off the sweat of your own father's back."

"Harve," I said, "you're talking like a Communist. It's mom who works, not dad."

"At a card table. Around disgusting men . . . come on."

My nose started to twitch like an Easter bunny. I was always nervous around Harve.

"Come on."

And I had to go down the hill again. Harve wasn't like the three fakers in their tower. I could press my advantage against Samson, Luke, and Mur, mount an attack. But Harve didn't have the same reclusive cunning or greed. He was like a trapper in some universe that was much more noble than mine. I could sing my way out of the worst situation. But Harve wouldn't warble. He went right for the throat.

He barged into the casino. Dubbie smiled when she saw him, rushed over to Harvey, put her arms around him, and little Marve danced near his feet. But mom was cautious. She knew the liabilities of having him around.

"Harvey," she said, "didn't you ever hear of a telephone?"

"Mom, I called the main desk. But nobody would dare interrupt your game."

"Then they're selfish. I should have been able to talk to my son."

And mom introduced Harve to all her habitués. Fred R. Lions, who might have met him during the dentist's time. Sheriff Billy Trumps. The former King Farouk. And Stanislaus, who'd sent his wife and son back to Manhattan but couldn't seem to break away from the Swan . . . or his bottle of gin.

"My oldest," mom said. "We had to send him to Arizona, so he could breathe the desert air. But it's a mother's misfortune to become a stranger to her son."

And Faigele started to guzzle Stanislaus' gin. Her hands were shaking. Stanislaus himself had to call the cards.

"Deuce of diamonds . . . six of clubs."

Harve wasn't blind. He must have noticed the soft electric pull between Faigele and Lansky's mob lawyer.

"I think I'll visit dad," he said.

And the game turned glum. Harve disappeared, but that couldn't ease the damage. The dark lady dealt with hysteria in her eyes. She guzzled more gin. Not even Stanislaus could save her. He was like a drunken pirate ship, mom's own Black Swan.

We had a regular household, thanks to Harve. Faigele couldn't skip meals and delegate the cooking to Dubbie, her sister-cousin-niece and confidante. Before Harve arrived, Dubbie could dance til midnight, and Faigele would still be in the casino, a Fatima between her lips, and if one of Dubbie's gallants started to paw her, mom would only have to whistle, and Billy Trumps would hurl his hat at the swain and Stanislaus would shower him with gin. But the midnight revels had to cease with Harve in the house. He'd appear at the casino a little after eleven, and mom wasn't strong enough to combat his scowls. She'd give the game to another dealer, and Harve would escort her and Dubbie home.

The dark lady developed her own nervous habits, which she was able to hide with Fatimas and gin. It was dad who prospered. Harve would sit him at the head of the table, where Faigele usually sat when she could steal a few minutes from her gambling and eat with us. Now we were like a faithful little family. Faigele cooked, Dubbie served, and Harve washed the dishes, with Marve and me, while dad had his schnapps.

"Faigele," he said, "I'm beginning to like the Catskills."

Harve had become his partner, would spend half his time selling soft drinks with dad.

"Why should I slave? I'll buy out the concession. But who should I buy it from? Tell me the name of the owner."

"The Black Swan," mom said.

"That's not a person."

"The Black Swan is a tax shelter, an entity." Stanislaus must have been coaching mom.

"An entity?" dad said. "What's an entity?"

"A corporation that hides its assets or sinks them into hospitals and nursing homes."

"Then what can I do?"

"Pocket a little money from the till."

"But that's stealing."

"Sam," she mumbled, her head floating with gin. "You can't steal from an entity. One hand feeds the other."

"I don't care. I've never stolen in my life."

But my big brother was much more adaptable. He convinced dad to borrow from the concession and scribble a couple of promissory notes.

"But when will I have to pay back what I borrow?"

"Not until the Black Swan divests itself of its nursing homes . . . and that's probably never, Dad."

"Then it's still like stealing."

But he listened to Harve and took from the till. His little stand was doing famously on account of dad's new clientele. Girls from bungalow colonies within a mile of the Swan flocked to his stand. They were in love with Harve. But Arizona must have coarsened him. He began to romance the mistresses and wives of millionaire merchants, men who summered at the Black Swan and would only visit Monticello on the weekends. Or perhaps the mistresses and wives did most of the romancing, because Harve looked much older and mysterious than his age. Or perhaps they got a kick out of being with a fourteen-year-old boy.

Soon as he escorted Faigele and Dubbie home from the casino, he'd saunter back in a blue vest, without wearing a shirt, and cha-cha with a whole caravan of mistresses and wives.

Dad remained silent. Harve might have reminded him of his winters in Miami during the war, when he did his own dancing with señoritas who sailed in from Havana to comfort furriers like himself. But mom didn't have dad's memories.

"Darling," she said to Harve, with a poisoned smile. "Do they pay you, your women friends?"

"Sometimes, mom."

And whatever fear she had of Harve, she was still the dark lady. She slapped him.

"Then you're a gigolo," she said.

He wouldn't touch his cheek where the slap fell.

"But I don't drink gin with Meyer Lansky's lawyer . . . and play cards with a harem full of men."

And Harve went out of the bungalow to make his rounds of the Black Swan's summer wives. Dubbie, dad, and little Marve had gone to bed. I sat up with mom, while she drank out of a golden thimble that Stanislaus had given her.

"He hates me," mom said. "I abandoned him."

"Mom, mom, he would have died without the desert. What could you have done?"

"Moved with him to Arizona."

"And sacrificed dad and me?"

She gulped another thimble. "You?" she said. "You don't need anybody. You're like a bat that flies in the dark . . . you think your brother can gallivant for free? A husband will come back early and kill him."

"Never," I said. "Not Harve."

Mom had much more cleverness than me. One of the millionaires, Marius Berlin, who owned a piece of the Black Swan, was utterly insane about his mistress, a certain Millie, who loved to dance. Berlin had hired a bunch of eunuchs to dance with her, had paid them well. But she preferred Harvey Charyn. The eunuchs complained to the millionaire. He could have borrowed Lansky's gorillas. But he was shrewd enough not to involve the Little Man. He realized that Stanislaus was fond of Faigele, and he might risk upsetting Meyer's affairs. And so he hired a backwoods family, the Cornwalls, who lived on a farm behind the casino and had never heard of Jeffersonian democracy. The Cornwalls didn't go to school. Their youngest son, Cal, worked at the Black Swan. He had scars all over one side of his body. He'd been scalded as a boy. His own dad had hurled a huge pot of boiling water at him in a drunken rage. The scars were terrible to see. But Cal didn't hide them. He'd walk around in an open shirt. He was a handyman at the Swan, a year or two older than Harve. He wasn't as thickly muscled, but he had a litheness that was like steel wire with albino marks where the hot water had landed.

We'd become friends. He'd let me do a little hammering when he had to repair a broken porch. He'd oil my beebee gun, show me how to strip it with the turn of a single screw. He kept prophylactics in his pocket, but none of the summer wives would sleep with Cal, because of the scars he carried, because of the dead white skin. He slept with his own cousins, Cornwall girls who were fascinated by his albino marks.

"Baby," he said, with a crop of nails in his mouth as he hammered a porch to perfection, "what about a threesome?"

"Is that like an acrobatic act?"

"Sorta," he said. "You, me, and my cousin Kim. She's thirteen. I could lend you a Trojan. Kim says you're an amazing child."

"What's so amazing about me?"

"You can read and write."

"That's no miracle. I've been studying how to spell for six straight years."

"It's a miracle to her . . . and all your learning excites Kim."

"But I haven't met your cousin, Cal."

"We're woods people. We don't like to be seen. But I've told her stories about you."

"What's there to tell? I couldn't even strip a beebee gun without you, Cal."

"But you could write a letter to the President of the United States."

"Then why the hell don't the Cornwalls go to school?"

"Because Monticello is full of Communists . . . and kikes."

"But I'm a kike, Cal."

"I forgive you," he said.

"And you hammer nails at a kike hotel."

"That's understandable. The kikes have money, and we have none . . . will you say hello to cousin Kim?"

Cal must have been the Aladdin of the woods. Because a bony little girl materialized out of nowhere like a wraith. She could have been a backwoods Rita Hayworth. I still wouldn't have worn one of Cal's Trojans. I was in love with Milady.

"This is Jerome, the spelling champion," Cal said. "Should we go to Cornwall country? It's down the next hill."

"Calvin," that little girl said, "I could take off my knickers right here."

I'd never seen such a bawdy little girl. The summer wives were pious children compared to Kim. But Cal could tell that I had no desire to explore her knickers. Perhaps I wasn't brave enough to wander into Cornwall country. Cal waved his hand and Kim vanished from the porch.

"What about your own cousin?" he said.

I knew he was talking about Dubbie, but I pretended not to listen.

"The cutie with eyeglasses . . . I promise. I'll throw my rubbers into the stream. I'd just like to have a conversation with her."

"She's a scholar, Cal. She can recite Shakespeare."

"Well, why couldn't she recite Shakespeare to me? It's the scars, ain't it? She wouldn't talk to an uncultured hill-billy with an iguana's skin."

"I'll ask her," I said.

"You won't. You're a lying, smooth-tongued kike."

And he went off with his nails and his hammer. But he returned in half an hour.

"Didn't mean to insult you, Baby. You're the best little kike at the Black Swan. But I have misfortunate news. Pa's been hired to beat the brains out of your brother."

"Who hired him?"

"This pasha called Berlin. He means business. Please tell your brother to skedaddle. I'd hate to cripple him. The pasha said we could finish up by stapling your brother to a tree."

I ran to Harve. He was smoking on his bunk at the Hawk's Nest. Harve wasn't fond of Fatimas. Lucky Strike was the favorite brand of cigarettes at his asthmatic retreat in Tucson.

"Harve," I said, "you'll have to blow."

"What for? I'm having a royal time at the Swan."

"You won't for long. Marius the millionaire is coming after you. He must have heard about your cha-cha with Millie."

"Millie means nothing to me," Harve said. "She's a bagatelle."

I wasn't sure what a bagatelle was. But I knew it had something to do with wearing Trojans in the middle of the afternoon.

"He's hired the Cornwalls to disfigure you."

"That family of dirt-road runts?"

"Harve, they're professional disfigurers. Mr. Cornwall ruined the body of his own boy."

"I'm staying," he said. "And don't you breathe a word to mom . . . or I'll disfigure you."

"Then keep away from Millie."

"I'll try. But I'm not responsible for Millie's actions. She can't stand to be touched by Berlin. She told me so."

I ran to the casino, signaled to Stanislaus. He put down his cards and brought his gin bottle over to my table. He could barely accomplish that little stroll.

"Stannie," I said, "you have to call the Little Man."

"He's in Havana. At the Nacional. It's a bigger palace than the Swan. Meyer lost his gambling rights. He's trying to get them back."

"But the Cornwalls are gonna massacre my brother."

"He shouldn't dance with rich men's fiancées. Who

hired them? Marius Berlin . . . I can't ask Meyer to intervene in Monticello affairs. I'm judge and jury at the Swan . . . convince your brother to get on a bus."

"He won't leave."

Stanislaus' chin fell against his chest. He was married to his gin bottle. I rushed to the hotel's abandoned barn. Tyrone was desolate. I'd forgotten to bring him food.

"Ty," I said, "my brother Harve's in trouble. The Cornwalls are promising to staple him."

I didn't have to explain the Cornwalls to Ty. Those dishwashers that had tried to rob him were part of the Cornwall clan.

"You expect me to break my cover? The Cornwalls are after me. And so is Sheriff Trumps. I'll have to rot in jail, or spend my life fixing ice-cream sodas for Meyer and his gang."

I couldn't save my brother. And I wouldn't let Tyrone see me cry. But I hadn't stopped scheming. I went to the casino with Dubbie and mom, waited for Harve to arrive. Meanwhile I cornered my cousin between dances.

"Dubbie," I said, "you have to come back after Harve declares his curfew."

"I would, but it will make your mother unhappy."

"You'll make her unhappier if you don't come. I swear. Just follow Harve and mom to our bungalow, brush your teeth, but don't get undressed. And after Harve leaves, you leave. Promise?"

"I promise," she said. And that was good enough for me.

Harve returned to the casino in his dancing vest. I prayed
that Millie had stomach cramps and couldn't do the cha-
cha that night. But I hadn't counted on her need for Harve.
It was a Wednesday night, and she didn't have to feel any
danger. Or perhaps it was danger that she wanted. I didn't
have an entrée into Millie's heart. She wore a red gown
with little shoulder straps. She was gorgeous, I have to admit. But she didn't have mom's fierce beauty, a beauty that
was independent of any man. Millie's eyes fluttered. Her
body moved with Harve's. She was like a strange, enrap-
tured bird. But that rapture didn't last.

Marius Berlin made his Wednesday night entrance,
flanked by Cornwalls: Kip, the father of the clan, with
white, white hair and one glass eye; Cal and three of his
older brothers, who were as belligerent as their dad, and
had the same horrific backwoods mien.

My heart thumped. The band stopped playing. I
watched the musicians pack their clarinets while the dancers
stood in place, except for Harve, who continued to cha-cha
with his own internal beat. Who the hell had raised him?
Some tribe of Arizona outlaw monks? There was no fear,
no hesitation, in his steps. Harve had leaped beyond the
Bronx, which, wild as it was, had its own law of prudence.

Millie was shivering in my brother's arms; she'd faint
in another minute.

Marius Berlin approached the dancing couple. I

couldn't recognize his tailor. He was wearing a scarlet shirt that didn't have the quiet, manicured look of Feuerman & Marx. How could I have guessed that he was a haberdasher? His millions had come from manufacturing shirts that blazed with the color of blood.

He could afford to be polite with the Cornwalls behind him. "Young man," he said, "I believe you're dancing with my fiancée."

Cal moved closer to Harve, and that's when he saw Dubbie Yellin in the casino, and he froze, like the other dancers, but the scars on his body did their own nervous dance.

I couldn't find the sheriff. Billy Trumps wouldn't hold cards when mom wasn't at her table. And Stanislaus sat in a drunken stupor.

Berlin slapped Millie. She started to sway. The straps fell off her shoulders, and she had to hold up her gown.

"Whore," Berlin said. Harve wouldn't withdraw like the the other swains who conducted summer romances at the Swan. He lifted the straps of Millie's gown and without losing a beat of his cha-cha, he slapped the millionaire.

Berlin was in a fury, but Kip Cornwall smiled.

"Son," he said to Harve, with the silkiness of a backwoods snake. "I'd rather not soil the casino with your guts. Will you be a gentleman and accompany us outside?"

"I'm not a gentleman," my brother said. "I'm a farmer like you . . . I grow desert grapes."

"Well, that's encouraging. We'll have to fight farmer to farmer. Mr. Berlin, will you give us a little room?"

He twirled the millionaire, spun him out of his way, and winking at his four boys, he prepared to jump on Harve. But a voice shot out at him like Satchel Paige's hesitation pitch.

"Is that hillbilly odds, five to one?"

It was the caid of Boston Road, who couldn't live in a barn when there was a battle nearby, no matter how many sheriffs were after him.

Kip rubbed his chin and rejoiced. "Look who's come out of the dark? A colored firefly."

Tyrone broke through the Cornwalls' little circle and stood back to back with Harve. He was clutching my digger.

Kip mocked the caid. "Boys, he's gonna blind us with that toothpick."

And that's when the sheriff appeared. I wondered if Billy Trumps had been waiting in the manager's room all this time and rehearsing his own little act . . . with the help of Stanislaus, who suddenly seemed in less of a stupor.

"Butt out of this, Billy," Kip said. "Take the nigger and go."

"Can't," said Billy Trumps.

"It's the Cornwalls what elected you . . . not the summer kikes."

"But you don't pay the bills."

Marius Berlin came out of his angry dream. "Sheriff, I demand justice."

"And what justice is that?"

"This gypsy boy has been trespassing . . . do you encourage common seducers at the Black Swan? He took advantage of my fiancée. Didn't he, dear?"

"Yes," Millie squealed. "I think so."

"She some kind of teenager, huh, Marius?"

"Careful, Billy. Remember, I'm associated with the Little Man."

"And I'm his *avocat*," said Stanislaus.

"I'll sell my interest in this mousetrap if I don't get some satisfaction," said Berlin. "I'm Meyer's haberdasher."

"All right, all right," said Billy Trumps, scratching his ear. "Kip, select one soldier."

"What the hell does that mean?"

"One soldier. A fair fight. I'll countenance that."

Kip's older sons rushed at him. "Pa, Pa," they said. But Cornwall wouldn't even give them the benediction of his glass eye. "Calvin," he said, "you take care of that romancing kike."

Dubbie wanted to rescue Harve from the Cornwalls. I had to hold her back.

"If you rush in, they'll only grab him outside the casino. Dubbie, they're diabolic . . . Harve will win. I promise."

She clutched my hand, while Harve and Cal began to pace the casino floor. They lunged. Harve ripped off Cal's shirt, revealing the albino blotches and marks that were like a riddle no one could really read. They lunged again, and Harve lost his vest. His muscles glowed under the dim casino lights, and he looked more godlike than ever.

They could have been a pair of gladiators, performing for a summer crowd of gamblers, gigolos, lusty wives, and one lone millionaire, Marius Berlin, the haberdasher who'd thrust himself into the Black Swan's weeknight rhythms.

Harve and Cal socked and scratched. Blood began to fly, and my cousin didn't want to watch.

"It's awful," she said. "It's like living in a house of cannibals."

"Dubbie," I pleaded. "The cannibals won't last."

And I was correct. Cal couldn't keep himself from looking Dubbie's way. And while he looked, Harve delivered a punch that propelled Cal into his own brothers, who barked like dogs and shoved him back into the fray. But Cal had lost his momentum and his wish to destroy Harve. I had him hooked. Harve kept punching him. But my brother didn't enjoy the fight. He followed Cal's constant gaze and discovered the object of his desire. He stopped dancing. Cal knocked him down. Harve wouldn't get up. Billy Trumps raised Cal's arm.

"The winner," Billy said.

Cal's brothers tried to carry him out of the casino. He wiggled away from the Cornwalls. He was still looking at Dubbie, who bent over Harve and wiped the blood off his face with a corner of her skirt. And Cal left the battlefield without his brothers.

"Billy," Kip Cornwall said, staring at Tyrone. "Ain't you gonna arrest the firefly?"

"No," Billy said, staring at Stanislaus.

"Then lend him to me."

"Not tonight. Take your boys and go on out of here. The Black Swan ain't Cornwall country. Not yet."

The caid of Boston Road had become an invisible man again. Meyer didn't seem to want him dead. Harve got up and shook Ty's hand.

"Mr. Harvey Charyn," the caid said, "it was a pleasure to watch you box."

And Ty went back to his barn.

Billy Trumps had to waltz around that haberdasher who was close to the Little Man and owned shares in the Black Swan. He banished Harve from Monticello "and all its environs," he said. My brother could have his last night at the Hawk's Nest, and then Billy himself would chauffeur Harve out of Sullivan County.

Sergeant Sam couldn't stop crying. "We found you and lost you again."

"It's all right, dad. But I hate to leave you alone with all that celery soda."

Faigele was like a sleepwalker. She kept fondling the

bruises on Harve's face and wiping blood that was no longer there.

"I'll be fine, mom. But I'd like to talk to Baby."

He took me up into the attic of the Hawk's Nest, shut the door, and started shaking me. "You fixed the fight, didn't you? Cal's in love with Dubbie, and you arranged it so she could watch me brawl."

"Harve, it was the only leverage I had."

He slapped me with the back of his hand, like he'd slap a child.

"I didn't need any leverage. And you would have shamed Cal in front of his family if I hadn't caught on. You're not my brother. You're a conniving little rat."

"But Harve, I wanted to help."

He twisted my ear. "I would have preferred a beating." And he walked out of the attic. . . .

It was lonesome without Harve. Dubbie wouldn't dance, and dad neglected the celery soda. He didn't even take from the till. And mom couldn't keep her mind on poker. She began to deal less and less. Rusty, the manager, was miserable. He couldn't earn a profit without mom at the tables. Big-time gamblers began to desert the Black Swan. Fred R. Lions would float across the casino. "Where's Faigele? Where's Faigele?"

But mom had exiled herself to the Hawk's Nest with a bottle of gin. She packed wads of money inside her brassiere, because she didn't trust Monticello banks.

"Why did I become the queen of poker?" she asked Dubbie and herself. "Why did I sit and sit until I couldn't see the color of a card? With all those men staring at me . . . it was to save for my children, to bring Harvey back to us, so he wouldn't feel like a foreigner."

"Mom," I said, "he loves Tucson."

"Good. And when will we see him again? In twenty years?"

"But maybe it's better if his visits are short and sweet."

Dad started to chase me around the bungalow. "Better for us . . . or better for you?"

"Sam," mom said. "Leave him alone. It's not Jerome's fault. It's another country, this Arizona."

"Arizona," little Marve muttered, inconsolable. Harve had brought him trinkets, bones and arrowheads from ancient burial grounds. Harve had carried him on his shoulder, into the Black Swan's orchards and deer park that didn't have a single deer. Harve had pampered him, while I was in the thick of some plot.

Little by little we returned to our old routines. My nose stopped twitching. Mom painted her eyes and went back to poker. The Swan began to pull in crowds from the other casinos. Rusty sang to himself, his head swollen with numbers.

But a peculiar weather seemed to invade the Swan, a heat that was so dense I could sock mosquitoes out of the air. It wasn't only mosquitoes. The Black Swan had tilted under my feet. It was a different hotel. For one thing, we were deprived of Stanislaus . . . and his stability. He'd fled the Swan, without leaving a note to mom or his little protégé. Perhaps Meyer had beckoned him from Havana, and Stanislaus had to run to the Hotel Nacional. Or else he'd gone back to Helen and Leicester and the obligations of a law firm. But he'd been mom's anchor at the card table, and her shield, and when gangsters approached her now, tried to get fresh, I was the one who had to whisper in their ear. "Sir, you're bothering the Black Swan, Meyer's fiancée." And if that didn't work, mom would toss in the cards and leave the table until the gangsters begged mom to return and promised to kill any of their own companions who wasn't polite to the Black Swan.

But I couldn't replace Stannie in mom's affections. I couldn't drink gin with her. And I sensed something sinister. Billy Trumps himself had abandoned mom's table. Fred R. Lions skulked back to the Bronx. Gangsters showed up at the casino, sat on their haunches like hyenas, smiled to themselves, and some of them didn't even gamble. Were they preparing to rape the Catskills, turn it into their own landlocked Little Havana?

"Mom, we have to get the hell out of here."

"And do what, my darling son? Waste away in the Bronx? Your father can't find a job. In Monticello we have food, money, fresh air."

"Mom, haven't you noticed? The mosquitoes are biting us to pieces."

"Then I'll buy a mosquito net. But don't rule my life."

And so I hunted with my beebee gun, and gathered food for Tyrone. But he wasn't inside his abandoned barn. He'd left my digger near the bundle of horse blankets that had served as his sleeping bag. The caid was signaling to me: take the digger and run. But how could I disappear without Dubbie, mom, dad, and little Marve?

I searched for Calvin Cornwall. He'd given up hammering, had quit the Black Swan. And so I took my Red Ryder, gathered all the courage I could, and went down that dirt road to Cornwall country. The Cornwalls didn't have orchards or a deerless deer park. They had their own woods and a ragged path that not even a tank could penetrate. I had to climb and claw over broken trees and wild plants that ripped my socks and left burrs in my shoes I couldn't shake out. I arrived at the Cornwalls with a limp, like a wounded veteran of some backwoods war. Their cabin didn't have the depth or the whiteness of our bungalow. It was a collection of chimneys and walls without windows. It didn't even have a porch. And I could only calculate with the snobbishness of a Bronx democrat: Tom Jefferson had never reached this part of the wilderness and never would.

Kip Cornwall stumbled out of the cabin in a pair of men's knickerbockers: pants cut off at the knees. He was clutching a deer rifle that was twice as large as my Red Ryder.

"We don't welcome dwarfs with beebee guns . . . not from the Black Swan. I'll give you three to run."

Then I heard Cal from inside the cabin. "Pa, that's a particular friend of mine. Leave him alone."

"Calvin, I'll break his bones and yours."

And Cal came out, wearing amputated pants, like his dad. His face was purple from Harve's punches. His cheeks were puffy. He walked right into the range of his dad's rifle and ignored him.

"Baby, would you care for a little country lemonade?"

"No refreshments," Kip said.

Cal pulled a jug out from beneath a knobby bench, and we both drank from it. Cornwall lemonade was like nothing I'd ever tasted: tangy, with whole chunks of lemon and pieces of bark. I was addicted to that lemonade after the first swallow. But Kip couldn't bear to see us have a little pleasure. He shot the jug right out of Cal's hands. It exploded and splashed Cal with lemonade. But Cal didn't react to the bomb Kip had created. That's what the world was like without Jeffersonian democracy. Lawless and crazed.

"Come, Baby," Cal said, and we walked into the jungle growth.

"Cal," I said, "I tricked you . . . I brought Dubbie down to the casino so you wouldn't have a clear conscience and be able to fight."

"It's only natural," he said. "You were protecting your brother. Against five cowboys. Wouldn't call that a fight."

"But I'm glad you won, Cal."

"Won? It was like clowning for strangers. I hope your

cousin don't think poor of me. Doing a millionaire's dirty work."

"But why aren't you up at the Swan hammering porches together?"

"Would be like hammering for Berlin. It's his kind what owns the Swan. Millionaires."

"Cal, will I ever see you again?"

"Doubt it," he said. "If you come calling, pa will sic the dogs after you, and my brothers will build a bonfire with your bones."

The gangsters were everywhere. And my three cellar rats came out of their dome. Mur didn't have any shame. He wiggled around like Hedy Lamarr and flirted with the gangsters, who saw him as an enigma, neither a woman nor a man, and avoided Murray Bell. But he took over the casino, turned it into a cabaret. He didn't dare strip at the Black Swan, which wasn't a community of howling, hungry sailors. The gangsters all had mistresses and wives. But Murray Bell did Delilah, and he danced his heart out, imprisoned in all his clothes.

The gangsters didn't know whether to laugh or cry. I appealed to Ev.

"Mur's embarrassing himself . . . and the Swan."

"Mind your business."

"But couldn't you drive him to Union City?"

"Mur wouldn't perform on his holiday," Samson said.

"Then why is he performing here?"

"For his own delight," said Luke. "For his own delight."

"But he'll flirt with the wrong gangster and get himself killed."

"There are no gangsters at the Black Swan," Samson insisted.

And I knew we were near the end of something. Monticello had become the land of the blind. Dubbie couldn't leave the Hawk's Nest without one or two gangsters following her around. And mom had to depend on the gallantry of former King Farouk. The gangsters' livelihood depended on Fatso Levine. They all had a percentage of his celery tonic routes. And if Fatso died defending mom, that would leave a hole in their pockets. But the oppressive heat brought out Fatso's megalomania. And he hurled Shakespeare at the gangsters, like King Richard. "Villains, lick my boots."

They kicked him down the hill. Dubbie and mom had to feed him and wash his face.

And that's when Stanislaus materialized. In the middle of Delilah's floor show. "Baby," he whispered. "Tell Faigele to pack."

"She's dealing, Stannie."

"Then you deal for her."

"But I'm not a pro. I couldn't call out the cards."

"Don't argue," he said. And he wasn't playing Joe Morse or John Garfield.

I sat at mom's table, signaled to her, and said, "Faigele, I'll deal."

Mom got up and walked out of the casino. I sat with the gangsters, who didn't play rough with me. I was the dealer, and they respected the rules. I tried to catch the lilt of mom's voice. But I wasn't sexy enough. My nose began to twitch. I stuttered when I called out the cards. One of the gangsters, who had a thick white scar over his eye, brought me a glass of celery soda. He was their caid, I imagined. Because the others were jittery around him.

"Will," they said, while he was pouring the soda into a large glass. "This kid could be a spy . . . the Little Man saved him from a jail sentence. That's what I heard on the street."

"The street," Will said, totally contemptuous. "Baby's all right. He's a tough customer."

And Will clinked glasses with me.

"He hangs around with niggers, Will. He's Tyrone Wood's best little man."

"That makes him a lot more reliable than a monkey like you."

I had a champion. And I didn't know the first thing about him, except that he was fond of celery soda.

"Will, he's in Stannie's camp."

"So are we."

"But you didn't say that yesterday, Will."

"Yesterday's a year ago. Now shut up. And let Baby deal."

My stutter disappeared. I sang out the cards. The gangsters stuffed money into my shirt, and I almost wished I had a banker's brassiere, like mom.

The musicians began to warm up in their little bandstand. I must have been high on celery tonic, because their instruments looked just like my plastic clarinet from P.S. 61. And then Delilah appeared, in a silver bodice, with trinkets on his arms.

The gangsters booed, but a single frown from Will was enough to silence them.

"Let the little lady do her dance."

"That's not a lady, Will. That's a goddamn fageroo."

"She's still Delilah in my black book."

And Delilah danced. The musicians played "Somebody Loves Me." But the casino itself was on a crazy tilt. Delilah's wig began to slide. His baubles made an awful bang that disrupted the sound of the band. But Delilah was irresistible. His bodice rose and fell. He moved his arms and legs like the most powerful temptress in Monticello. Will and his men were hypnotized . . . until the sheriff crashed right through the window with his own little band.

"Will Scarlet, you're under arrest."

Will turned over the card table.

The sheriff laughed. "Are you really gonna fight us, Will?"

And that's when a hand plucked me from my chair. It belonged to Stanislaus. He carried me between the warring parties and out of the casino.

"Stannie," I said, "who's Will Scarlet?"

"Meyer's mortal enemy."

"But what does it all mean? I drank celery soda with him."

"He's promiscuous," Stanislaus said. "He could share a glass with you and blow your head off."

And then Stanislaus tossed me into his limo, which was packed with Charyns and Dubbie Yellin.

"What about Farouk?"

"Is he family?"

"No, but . . ."

"Baby," mom said, "be quiet."

And we drove off Monticello's little mountain.

That was fifty years ago. And now I have my own Hawk's Nest, above the bones of Baudelaire and Beckett, Ionesco and Alekhine, the Russian chessmaster who lived in Paris during the war and was the Nazis' alcoholic darling. And why do I dream of Will Scarlet's face? I met him once, for less than an hour. He was as anonymous as any gangster, but that flight from the Black Swan was like some movement into my own anonymity, as if my future had collapsed. I never saw Tyrone Wood again. I walked Boston Road, but not a soul would give me news about the caid. Fatso disappeared from the Chesterfield with his own brand of celery soda. He couldn't outlast the White Rock Girl.

I visited the Luxor, but I couldn't find my cellar rats. I went to Engine 42. Dan O'Brien had been transferred to some phantom company that the other firemen wouldn't tell me about. I sank into a crippling form of amnesia, the disease of Dubbie's archipelago. But she would have a certain victory. Black students managed to wade across the Bronx River and attend James Monroe, just as the Morris Mothers finally convinced City Hall to send white boys and girls to Morris High. I like to think that Tyrone, dead or alive, had been the angel who brokered that deal. Dubbie would fall in love and get married a little after Monticello, but she'd had scarlet fever as a child (the fever had damaged her heart), and she would die young, giving birth to a little boy. We all mourned her, but Faigele couldn't recover. Dream daughters are hard to find. I loved her too, and she was the only one in my whole life who never looked at me with the least bit of caution. I was Faigele's child, and that was enough for Dubbie. I could feel the force of her smile in Stanislaus' limousine.

It had begun to rain, but the real electric storm was inside that car. Little Marve sat on dad's lap. Faigele sat with Dubbie, their arms laced around each other. Stanislaus and I were on the jump seats, facing Faigele. He couldn't survive that gangland war. The Little Man would live into his eighties, running from Manhattan to Cuba to Israel and Miami Beach. But Stanislaus had nowhere to run. He was found in the trunk of his own limousine a few months after our trip, with a bullet in his brain. I saw the bullet hole on the cover of the *Daily Mirror*. He didn't look agonized. He was in the middle of some luckless dream.

But Stanislaus wasn't dreaming as we drove down from Monticello. The rain on the roof could have been a massive heartbeat that belonged to the car, as if we were all breathing to some profound rhythm that was larger and more immediate than any one of us. I had a devil in me, some serpent who'd broken out of Monticello's little Eden. Because I wanted to annihilate Sergeant Sam. I had a long scroll of grievances. He'd gassed my little dog. He'd locked me in the closet. He wouldn't come to Simpson Street, save me from the bulls. But the problem was, how to kill him and keep him alive? I was a different kind of murderer than Will Scarlet or that Richard with the hump on his back. I wasn't after territorial rights. It was Stanislaus. He was the dad I desired. And it's a terrible sin to feel like a changeling in front of your own father. Kill him and keep him alive.

Stanislaus put his arm around me. He avoided Faigele. He couldn't look at mom while Dubbie, Marve, and dad were there. But Faigele blushed with the remorse of rain on a roof. She was Stanislaus' black swan. How could they speak in the car? What language would they have used? Farouk had memorized Shakespeare while he was in a bamboo cage. Words had delivered him from death. But not all of Shakespeare's sound and fury could have delivered Stanislaus. It was mom, only mom, who had the magic to make the unspeakable speak. She lit her last Fatima, shared it with Stanislaus . . . like a rose on fire. Did I realize that Stanislaus would disappear so soon? I clenched my fists and begged God that we could ride and ride in the rain, outrun Monticello and gangland deaths, with mom and her Fatima. But the Fatima went out, and I could see the dark coal in Stannie's eyes.

Jerome, the future JD, a little after the events of this book.

NOTE TO THE READER

Although this memoir was inspired by the experiences of my childhood, certain characters, places, and incidents portrayed in the book are the product of imaginative re-creation and these re-creations are not intended to portray actual characters, places, or events.